THE
PIAZZA

Stories from Piazza Santa Caterina Piccola

BOB BRUSH

illustrations by
SCOTT HOWARD

THE STORIES

THE
PIAZZA

Stories from Piazza Santa Caterina Piccola

Per Mel
La Mia Compagna,
La Mia Vita

PIAZZA SANTA
CATERINA PICCOLA

If it is true that each memory casts a shadow forever, let one shadow be that of a boy.

The boy stands in the center of a busy square beneath a summer sun. He is eight years of age. Around him there is noise and dust, the rattle of horses and carts, chickens and goats, hawkers and vendors, argument and opinion; the joyous gabbling of life in a place that no longer exists, if it ever existed at all.

The square is, was, called Piazza Santa Caterina Piccola, on the outskirts of Monte Castella, a small Italian hill town up the road from a much larger town from which a railroad leads to the great cities of Rome, Milan, and Naples. Narrow streets wind down the hill to the cobblestoned piazza, which is encircled by shops: a bakery, a barbershop, a *macelleria*, a *caffè*. There is a hotel, the Grand Hotel Imperiale, built in a folly of optimism years before but still, beneath its flags, the proud emblem of a certain sardonic civic pride. Across the square stands a Church – Catholic, naturally – and, in its shadow a small stone shelter.

The year is 1933.

There is a movie theater, recently renamed *Cinema Duce* in honor of Rome's latest candidate for immortality, Benito Mussolini; and a statue of Giuseppe Garibaldi, beneath which lies the town well, where anything important – or anything not – is discussed, dissected, and ratified by the women who come to do laundry.

There are still more horses than automobiles, more rumors than telephones, more goats than politicians. There are no soldiers.

Not yet.

In the center of this is the boy, standing on his shadow. His name is Niccolò. He lives above the bakery, which is run by his mother and his grandfather since Niccolò's father left for America in search of a new life for them all. Niccolò was born here. This place is his world. Years from now, when the town of Monte Castella has vanished in a conflagration of politics and war, he will remember the stories of the people and things that were here.

He will remember life and death, love and remorse, the unutterable magic of a very small place in a perilous time.

Piazza Piccola is where everything in these stories took place.

All of it happened.

None of it is true.

NONNO

Everyone knew everything about everyone else on Piazza Piccola, or thought they did, which was very much the same thing. From Mamma's bakery window the boy Niccolò could, in the course of a day, account for most of the local populace as they crossed the square, enacted their business, argued, laughed, pulled their suspenders, stroked their beards, made threats, shook hands and, when the occasion called for it, lied. Behind each face lurked a story, only occasionally based on fact, which forever defined its owner. Thus Libertini the iceman was famous for having six fingers on one hand, Morelli the vegetable seller for talking to his horse. Biggio the barber's great uncle was Giuseppe "Joe the Boss" Masseria, who died in a blast of gunfire on Coney Island, an ace of spades clutched in his poker hand. Who did not know that the Widow Petacci once sat behind Greta Garbo on a bus in downtown Naples? Or that Bruno Fabbro the stablemaster kept the sayings of *Il Duce* on his nightstand?

To which Nonno, Niccolò's grandfather, applied the old proverb '*Chi bestia va a Roma bestia ritorna*' – "He that goes to Rome a fool returns a fool."

Nonno, Niccolò was certain, was anything but a fool.

To Niccolò it seemed his grandfather, who had been alive forever and surely would always be, was the wisest man on Piazza Piccola, therefore in Italy, therefore on earth. Barely five feet high with hands like iron sledges, Nonno worked in the bakery six days a week, hauling sacks of flour and tending the oven while Mamma dealt with the customers, kept the books and ran the shop.

At night Nonno slept on a palette in the storeroom, snoring uproariously and shouting in his sleep. Sundays, as the Bible suggested, he rested (he had no use for the Church), sitting by the radio smoking and shaking his head at the news from Rome. And although he was hardly a conversationalist ("*Belle parole non pascon i gatti*" – "Fine words don't feed cats," he would snort), in the case of his grandson he made an exception. With Niccolò on his knee, Nonno would tell of growing up in a place not so far distant, yet in customs and people a universe apart from the sunlit world of Mamma's bakery; of his life as a blacksmith, then a soldier, a prizefighter, even an acrobat. To Niccolò, Nonno's life read like a storybook: exotic, burly and wild. The best part was when Mamma, listening, would *tsk* at the more colorful chapters, hiss at Nonno, bang the pots and send Niccolò to bed.

There were other things as well his grandfather taught Niccolò, things a father might have done, but Papà was for now an ocean away. Nonno showed Niccolò how to set traps for mice, whittle with a pocketknife and, when Mamma wasn't around, chew tobacco and pee in the sink. Once, when they discovered an abandoned litter of kittens beneath the stairs outside the storeroom, Niccolò begged Nonno to keep them - one in particular, a tiny male with a star-shaped mask. Nonno refused and drowned them in a vat of water. It was Niccolò's first lesson in cruelty and death and he made up his mind to hate his grandfather forever. But time went by and Nonno was kind, so eventually Niccolò forgave him and sat on his lap again, while Nonno told him the kind of things boys need to hear to become bigger boys. When Nonno spoke like this, Niccolo always listened.

Except when it came to the old man in the hat.

Two times a week that man – *il vecchio*, very old, perhaps close to a century – made his way down from the hill above the piazza, teetering on his cane, scraping his shoes and mumbling to himself, cursing angrily at all who greeted him. Inside his hat or sometimes pinned to his lapel he carried a list. Some called him *Senatore* though no one knew of him ever being such, while the more insolent young people, for whom respect was a burden, called him *Geppetto* after the puppet-maker in the tale of *Pinocchio*. But no one had any real idea as to who the old man was. Time had erased his past; he'd outlived his own story.

When he arrived at the bakery, often confused and upset, Mamma would smile and treat him with special care. She knew his grand-niece, with whom he lived. It was she who put the list in the old man's hat so it wouldn't get lost. Even so, it often did.

But while Mamma was busy showing the old man courtesy and respect, Niccolò and his friends, Quindici and Rinaldo, were not. As he stood at the counter they would hide out of sight and imitate his bent-over walk, his trembling hands, his toothless mumbling - though not his profanities, for that, had Mamma heard, would have resulted in mouthfuls of soap. When the old man teetered out, clutching his parcel of bread, the boys would poke each other and double over in giddy laughter.

Once, however, Niccolò saw Nonno at the storeroom door, watching as he and his friends made fun. Nonno shook his head slowly, but said nothing. Then, after dinner that night, while Mamma cleared the dishes, Nonno took Niccolò out to the sidewalk and pointed toward the statue of Garibaldi in the center of the square.

"*Sai chi è?*" he asked. "Do you know who that is?"

"*Sì,*" said Niccolò. "Garibaldi."

"Do you know what he did?"

Niccolò gave it some thought.

"Discovered America?" he offered.

Nonno dragged on his cigarette. His eyes wandered across the square to the *caffè*, where a group of young men in black shirts had recently taken to lounging, drinking beer and shouting *fascisti* slogans at passersby.

"That old man you mocked. He fought with Garibaldi. *Capisci?*"

"*Sì,*" said Niccolò, even though he didn't.

Nonno fixed Niccolò with a penetrating eye. "'*Qui si fa l'Italia o si muore,*'" he said. "'Here we make Italy or die.' Remember I told you this."

And the matter was dropped, unfortunately before Niccolo had time to determine precisely what the matter was.

In fact, the more he thought about it, the less he understood. What did an old man who pissed his pants have to do with anything?

Much less an old statue covered in pigeon droppings.

∽

THEN CAME AN EVENING when the old man once again made his way down the hill, and the day had been long, and the boys had grown tired of their games and had argued with each other and grown tired of that, and now they were restless and bored. As the old man passed they fell in behind him, imitating his rickety walk, mocking his mumbling, repeating his curses (this time Mamma was nowhere around). Across the square they danced behind him, marching, whistling, pretending to play the fifes, the trumpet, the drums. Quindici imitated a monkey, Rinaldo made the sound of farts. The more they did this, the more agitated the old man became, muttering in confusion, which only added to the hilarity of the boys.

As they passed the *caffè* the black-shirted men turned to watch. One shouted, "Go on! Give the old fool a lesson!" The others laughed. "Make him dance!" they shouted. Their laughter spurred the boys on.

The old man's hat fell off. Dizzy with silliness, Niccolò picked it up, put it on his own head and raced in circles, alive with the rapture of ridicule, the attention of the men, the pure joy of nonsense.

Then suddenly things weren't so funny.

The hand that seized his collar from behind clamped down like an iron vise. Terrified, squealing, Niccolò felt himself dragged across the piazza into the bakery and down the stairs to the storeroom. There Nonno, grim-faced and merciless, removed his belt. Niccolò yelped in fear; then cried out in pain as the belt came down on his buttocks, again and again.

It was the first time he had ever been beaten. Nothing before or after hurt as much.

9

Later, upstairs in the bakery Nonno dried Niccolò's tears and sat him on his knee. "Every welt on your butt is a gift I give you." he said. "Next time you think to make fun of a man, stop to rub your ass and remember this day." Which was why some days later when the boys once again commenced mocking the old man, Niccolò told them to stop and rub their asses.

Naturally, this required a response from the others.

"Rub your own ass," said Quindici.

"That's not how it works," said Niccolò.

"Why don't you rub it for me?" sneered Rinaldo, who had learned to sneer from his older brothers and was good at it.

Niccolò felt things getting away from him.

"Stay away from Niccolò, he'll rub your ass!" shouted Rinaldo.

"Niccolò likes to rub asses," giggled Quindici.

"Niccolò likes to rub asses," Rinaldo repeated delightedly, and with that the insult had wings. Across the piazza the two boys danced, forgetting the old man entirely, chanting their slander until their orbit brought them back to where they began.

"Well?" said Niccolò.

"*Sei un finocchio,*" said Rinaldo.

Niccolò kicked at Rinaldo, who swung at Niccolò's face, which turned into a fistfight which, by the time Morelli the vegetable seller broke it up, left Rinaldo with a bloody nose and Niccolò with a broken tooth and black eye.

Mamma raged and called Niccolò a ruffian, then turned on Nonno. "It's your fault," she hissed. Nonno kept his eyes down. Mamma washed Niccolò's face, swabbed his gums with basil tea and sent him to bed without supper. That night, Niccolò heard them arguing. "He'll grow up a savage," she cried.

10

"The world will soon be run by savages," replied Nonno. "At least he'll know how to survive."

After that it was quiet, but later Niccolò awoke to find his grandfather by his bed. Nonno took Niccolò's face in his big hands and Niccolò smiled through his broken tooth. Nonno pulled up his shirt to show Niccolò the scars from his days as a soldier, and kissed him on his forehead, and Niccolò knew he'd been forgiven.

"*Qui si fa l'Italia o si muore,*" nodded Niccolò.

Here we make Italy, or die.

As for the old man, the following year he disappeared in the ruins. No one knew what to make of it.

But Niccolò knew.

Fausto, the fool, told him.

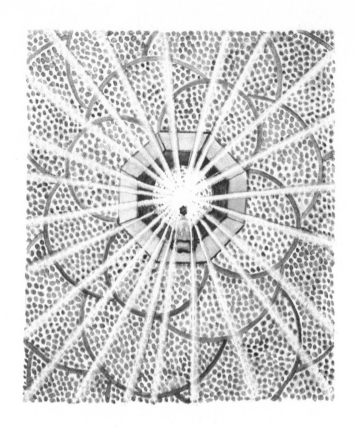

A MAN OF GOD

Monsignore Don Federico was, above all, a man of order. From disorder grew chaos, and chaos gave Don Federico boils.

To the venerable elder prelate of the Church of San Bartolomeo Giusto on Piazza Santa Caterina Piccola, order was the earthly manifestation of Heaven, the visible hand of God who in the beginning separated One Thing from the Other and pronounced it Good. Likewise, did Don Federico strive to hold back the tide of chaos in his own earthly domain. No matter if outside, in the dust and dung of the piazza, politics and quarrels filled the air; in the quiet haven of San Bartolomeo all was immaculate, things in their place. Even the statues of saints and martyrs lining the nave at measured intervals gazed outward in alabaster serenity, polished and shining, never mind their deaths had been gruesome bloodfests at the hands of demented mobs. To Don Federico, history was clutter, and Church – particularly his church - was no place for clutter.

So on Sundays, as the congregation - among them Niccolo and Mamma - gathered under the organizing principal of the bells, Don Federico, resplendent in his robes, intoned the order of the Mass, the heavenly rhythms of call and response, unaltered since the days of the catacombs. Woe betide the parishioner who dared to whisper, or shift in his pew. On Sundays, things ran like clockwork. On Sundays the Word of God prevailed.

On other days, things were not so simple.

Other days on Piazza Piccola there were other deities to attend to: superstitions, the bastard children of faith, whose unruly demands formed the lifeblood of Christian conduct in everyday life. To avoid disaster one did well to appease these demons as well as the Lord. Thus, salt over the shoulder brought luck. A knife in the dirt brought rain. A hat on the bed guaranteed death. Never shave on Friday, eat lentils at midnight on New Year's Eve, avoid a draft – *un colpo d'aria* – that could kill. A pregnant woman wore a key on her belly when the moon was full, to spare her child a harelip. Most dreadful of all, atop this Olympus of terror dwelt *Malocchio*, the evil eye, who lurked around every corner with gifts of death and misfortune. To even the most faithful, life was subject to the whim of miracles and signs. Nevertheless, in Don Federico's mind, so long as the faithful rendered unto God what was God's and left their demons at the church door, equilibrium was maintained. Which was good: from disorder came chaos. And chaos, as has been said, gave Don Federico boils.

So, as it happened, did Fausto.

To Fausto – the smiling, goggle-eyed, snaggle-toothed sweeper of dust and stones, demented guardian over all comings and goings in the piazza– to this half-witted fool God was a living, hovering Presence, benevolent when pleased, vengeful when provoked. God lurked among the fissures of the very stones that made up Fausto's small shelter in the shadows of the church, where children teased him by day and orphaned dogs sheltered at night.

There, while the town slept, God rampaged through Fausto's nightmares like an avenging Cossack, demanding not order but obedience, absolute, abject and craven. It was only natural, then, that on Sundays the church was to Fausto an altar on which to launch a desperate, direct appeal to his Deity. Let the rest of the flock observe decorum: Fausto's imprecations were guttural, the cry of a wounded animal. He mewled; he screeched; he bayed. From his seat high in the rafters his howlings swept across the pews and rattled past the Saints and Martyrs directly into the ears, and under the skin, of Don Federico, whose only strategy was to ignore them.

"*Credo in unum deum…*" the Monsignore intoned as the congregation kneeled.

"ABBI PIETA DI ME, SIGNORE!" came the moan from the back of the church.

"…*accípiens et hunc præclárum…*" persevered Don Federico, turning his eyes to heaven as the wine became blood.

"SANCTA MARIA! SALVAMI!" came the agonized howl of a soul teetering on the lip of damnation.

It was the same every Sunday.

It was enough to shake the patience of an Apostle; yet when, at the moment of communion, Don Federico stood at the altar rail looking down at this trembling wreck of rags kneeling before him, did he even once hesitate in his priestly duties? Did he even once, holding the wafer suspended, consider denying God's gift to a being so utterly wretched?

No. The shepherd tends to each lamb in the flock and loves them all. Accommodations could always be made.

Until the day the Archbishop's letter arrived.

WORD REACHED DON FEDERICO on his hands and knees in the rectory garden, separating peonies from nasturtiums. Flowers appealed to the Monsignore: they did what they were told.

"He's coming here?" he said, sitting up, to Father Tommaso, who was holding the letter. "When?"

Father Tommaso, who had recently arrived at San Bartolomeo and was junior to the Monsignore by some decades, consulted the text. "Six weeks from now. He's on his way to Pienza to consecrate an altar. He'll be here at noon, have a bite, say a Mass, and be on his way."

"He's coming for lunch?" asked Don Federico.

"That's what it says," replied the young priest.

"After which he'll be on his way?"

"So this would indicate," said Father Tommaso.

A visit from the Archbishop! It was an honor, even if it was just for lunch, even if it was because the archbishop required a place to rest his feet. The news filled the elder prelate with a celestial joy.

"You're standing in my nasturtiums," he said to Father Tommaso.

"My apologies," replied Father Tommaso, who was not by nature a gardener.

Instantly a plan took shape in Don Federico's mind. The church would be scrubbed, pews polished, saints and martyrs dusted and waxed. The Monsignore himself would come up with a sermon that might long be remembered, something to do with the sanctity of order as a bulwark against perfidy and sin. The thought occurred that perhaps he could persuade his flock to dress in matching colors; or failing that, in blacks and whites, creating a pleasurable checkerboard effect.

"That might be overdoing it." noted Father Tommaso, gently.

"Just a thought," said Don Federico, making a mental note of the younger priest's unhelpful attitude.

By evening the plan was complete. It would be the crowning achievement of Don Federico's tenure. He poured a glass of sherry, savored the moment, and went to bed.

At three in the morning he awakened.

"Fausto!" he uttered in horror.

Fausto! The nightmare rose up before him: the Mass going smoothly, Don Federico attending the Archbishop at the altar with chalice raised; then suddenly, horribly, from the choir loft – a shattering howl. Fausto! Startled, the Archbishop steps backward, and trips: the chalice slips from his hands, the wine splattering across his robes; a gasp from the congregation...

"*Abbi pietà di me, Signore!*" muttered the Monsignore, clutching his covers to his neck. There was no ignoring it: a fly had appeared in the ointment. To avert disaster, Fausto would have to be dealt with.

In the gray light of dawn, as Don Federico considered his options, was God gazing down?

16

"BLESS ME FATHER, for I have sinned," croaked Fausto the following Thursday in the confessional of St. Bartolomeo. It was the perfect place for a conversation. On Thursdays, from his seat behind the screen, Don Federico dispensed advice and absolution to all manner of sinners, adulterers and lonely hearts, including Signora Costa, the bricklayer's widow, whose favorite cow had wandered into the hills and not been heard from for weeks. Here, in the closet of God, difficult issues could be broached and resolved.

"My sins are these," began Fausto.

"We'll get to that," interrupted Don Federico. "First, a matter of importance."

"*Scusi?*" responded Fausto, perplexed by this change in the ancient litany.

"The Archbishop is coming," said the Monsignore.

Fausto frowned. "*Perché?*"

"Never mind why," said Don Federico. "He'll be saying Mass in this very church. It will be an occasion of great solemnity. Which is why..." he paused for effect, "...I shall need your cooperation."

Across the screen, Fausto hesitated. Was the Monsignore asking him to scrub the floors? "*Come?*" he asked, "How?"

Don Federico pounced, according to plan. "Keep quiet. Say nothing. Be silent," he said, then paused, awaiting the fool's response. None was forthcoming. "Well? Have you nothing to say?"

"You said to be silent," said Fausto, whose confusion was rapidly growing.

"Not now. At the Mass!" barked Don Federico.

17

"Which Mass?" bleated Fausto.

"All of them! Beginning immediately!" commanded Don Federico. It had suddenly struck him that here was an opportunity for a *coup de main*, a permanent solution to a long-standing thorn in his side. "It's high time this ridiculous caterwauling ceased."

There followed another long silence. Fausto's thoughts spun. People seldom discussed matters of importance with him, let alone a priest, let alone in the house of the Creator. Perhaps the Monsignore had him confused with someone else?

"*Sì, Monsignore*," he said.

Having killed two birds with one stone, Don Federico allowed his tone to soften; after all, he was not a tyrant. "It's simply a matter of self-control," he advised. "Worship, but with less gusto. Am I understood?"

Fausto blinked. "*Sì, Monsignore.*"

"Good!" boomed the priest, and clapped his hands. "Now, let's have a good Act of Contrition."

"What about my sins?" puzzled Fausto.

"Six Hail Marys, fifteen Our Fathers. There are people waiting." The screen snapped shut on Fausto. And the matter, thought Don Federico, was handled

Until Sunday.

"CRISTO, ABBI PIETA DI ME!" Cracked and desperate, the voice erupted with such anguish that even those in the foremost pews, who had grown used to it over the years, turned to look. Don Federico, at the altar, felt the first stirrings of discomfort beneath his skin. Had he not expressed his wishes clearly?

"Bless me father, for I have sinned," began Fausto the following Thursday in the confessional.

"Never mind that!" boomed Don Federico. "Did you forget? Or are you mocking me?"

Fausto remained silent, hoping for a clue.

"Perhaps I failed to make myself clear," continued Don Federico. Once again he laid out the situation - the Archbishop's pending visit, the need for best behavior - attempting to convey some of his deeply cherished philosophy on the importance of order while avoiding the odor of mildew emanating from Fausto's clothes. Fausto listened intently, brow furrowed, tongue dangling in concentration.

"So, are we understood? *Hai capito?*" said Don Federico, through the screen.

Fausto nodded his head vaguely. "*Ho capito.*"

But the following Thursday --

"Have you heard even one word I've said?" roared Don. The Archbishop's visit was fast approaching. "Or are you deaf?"

Across the confessional screen, Fausto cowered.

"Why," groaned the Monsignore in frustration, "do you insist on this raucous shrieking? Is your head full of wax?"

Suddenly the fool understood what the priest had been getting at. "But Monsignore," he said brightly, "it's how I speak to God."

"You don't <u>have</u> to speak to God! I do that for you!" thundered Don Federico. "Let God speak to <u>you</u>!"

Fausto had squeezed himself into a terrified ball in the corner of the confessional.

"If you refuse to restrain yourself," roared the priest, for the moment losing all sense of restraint, "you will not be allowed in the church at all."

"*Scusi?*" squeaked Fausto, now no more than a mouse.

"You heard me. No more talking to God! *Basta! Finito!*"

19

Certain at last that his message had been received, Don Federico once again slammed the screen shut and turned to the Widow Costa, whose cow had regrettably still not returned from the hills. For those who might suggest that the Monsignore's treatment of the fool was harsh – a denial of a most basic right of worship – one might consider that in the cause of order (the lack of which leads to chaos) stern measures are sometimes required. Add to that the fact that for Don Federico the Archbishop's visit meant more than a simple appointment for lunch. Here at last was a chance for the Monsignore to demonstrate the full range of his principles, to ratify a lifetime of struggle in the hinterlands of the Faith. The truth was that Don Federico had turned down offers of more central parishes for this feckless outpost on the edge of nowhere, a diocese he could mold in his own image. Perhaps now his decision would be redeemed. Assisting the Archbishop in saying Mass in the sublime and peaceful harmony of San Bartolomeo Giusto would be a pinnacle. The thought that anything might interfere made him want to cry.

While that night, in his stone hut in the piazza, Fausto sat shivering, terrified at the thought of being deprived of his weekly conversation with the Lord. Over and over the priest's words echoed in his head: "Let Him speak to you." But why would God, who ruled the heavens and commanded the stars and the oceans, in all His terrifying grandeur, bother to speak to an insignificant sweeper of stones? In despair Fausto hid himself under his blanket of newspapers and straw and, shooing away the mice, sniffled and went to sleep.

It was that very night he heard the voice in the well.

The voice was the voice of God.

Not so much a voice, perhaps, as a vibration in the air, profoundly resonant, that woke him after midnight and summoned him first to his

20

doorway, then across the cobbled square to the lip of the central well: a ragged figure moving as if in a trance beneath a canopy of stars, the smallest of specks in the vast, dismal reach of the universe. Once arrived at the well, he peeked in.

From below the glimmering surface, the voice spoke.

It spoke to Fausto directly, as Father to son. As Shepherd to sheep. As God to man. As it did, an invisible bolt of lightning, dark and powerful, stabbed upward from the depths through the dirt and filth that covered this improbable wraith and struck to the very center of his immortal soul. Or so it seemed to Fausto, transfixed at the edge of the well where by day took place the business of mortal commerce: the washing, the gossip, the petty jealousies, the betrayals, the secret hopes. Now, on this night, a greater commerce was being transacted.

God spoke to Fausto who, if he didn't understand it all, at least caught the gist. And when God had finished, Fausto fell like a stone to the ground.

Which is where they found him the next morning, stiff as an iron bar.

THE NEWS REACHED Don Federico in his bathtub, where he often lingered to contemplate Moses parting the sea. "It's the fool," said Father Tommaso, stepping into Don Federico's reverie. "He's had a fit."

"Where?"

"In the square. Last night." Father Tommaso hesitated. "He says he's spoken with God."

Don Federico set down his soap.

By the time he'd dressed and reached the piazza a crowd had gathered. In the early morning light the scene resembled one by Caravaggio: a knot of spectators surrounding a central figure, held upright in the arms of a few awestruck witnesses, tunic torn, his eyes glittering with the pure light of revelation. Untended goats wandered in all directions.

"He was dead when I found him," explained Donati the goatherd, who had first stumbled upon Fausto lying stiff on the cobblestones. "But when I knelt down, he came to life."

"Like Lazarus," exclaimed Vittorio Menucci, who had been opening his *caffè* and had witnessed it from across the square. Around the group there were nods. A sheep bleated. Don Federico, wishing he were still in his bath, held up a hand.

"First," he announced, "let me speak to the man."

"*Che Dio ti benedica,*" cried Fausto, rising unsteadily from the grasp of his neighbors. "God has called to me."

Don Federico rolled his eyes. "Where?"

Fausto raised a finger toward the well. All eyes followed his; in the early sunshine the well seemed to glow, as if newly remade. The Widow Petacci, standing nearby, took a step back and crossed herself, as did everyone else; everyone but Don Federico,

"God," he said patiently, "does not speak from wells."

"He spoke to Moses from a bush," suggested Biggio the barber, who had just arrived on the scene.

"That was different," said Don Federico, not pleased to be challenged on matters of doctrine. "A bush is not a well. And this addle-brain is certainly not Moses."

The point was well made. Possibly Don Federico should have left it there.

"And what is it, exactly," he said instead to Fausto, "that you imagine God told you?"

Fausto cocked his head, as if hearing the Words once more. An enormous grin, all the more joyful for its toothlessness, spread across his crooked face as it came to him, the profound and amazing truth. "*Tutti!*" he shouted. Just as suddenly the grin disappeared, replaced by a look of sheer terror, as if feeling within himself an alien presence. "*Quae prima fuerunt, ecce: venerunt ...*" he blurted.

There were gasps from the crowd, which was growing by the minute. Clearly, this was an event. Foolishness from Fausto was one thing, conjugating Latin quite another.

"*Ego adnuntio,*" whispered Fausto, looking from one astonished face to the next, his own just as astonished. "*Audita vobis faciam.*"

From the onlookers came a shriek. The *Signora* Felice Di Pasqua, who cleaned rooms at the Grand Hotel Imperiale and hadn't missed mass in thirty-three years, pushed her way forward. "It's from the Bible. Isaiah," she cried. "It means he's been given the Vision!"

A chorus of murmurs mixed with the bleating of sheep, who were by now scattered all over the square. Never mind those very words of Isaiah had been the subject of the Monsignore's sermon two Sundays previously. Perhaps no one had paid attention; perhaps they had forgotten. Don Federico assessed the situation: on one hand the innocent ravings of a lunatic could be dismissed as harmless; on the other blasphemy was blasphemy, even from the mouth of a fool. He raised a hand to staunch the murmurs.

"Enough!" he announced "Let this lunacy cease!"

"Beware," shouted Fausto, at the top of his lungs, "lest your fields be ravaged by crows."

"Everyone off to their business!" commanded Don Federico.

"Take not for granted the evening star, lest it fail to light your path," howled Fausto; then, pointing a finger in the direction of Poggio the tailor, "If you would seek treasure, look no further than beneath your own dwelling." Poggio, who had only just arrived on the scene, frowned as if accused. Fausto turned in the direction of Morelli the fruit seller. "Your wife is with child," he announced. "A female child."

"Tell me something I don't know," said Morelli, who already had eleven daughters and not one son. Morelli's horse, who it was rumored could talk, simply shook its head.

Fausto did not hesitate. "Your horse will throw a shoe this very afternoon," he said.

"Where is my cow? Is she safe?" called Signora Costa, the bricklayer's widow.

The Monsignore considered his options. A situation like this, with the Archbishop due in two weeks, was redolent of disorder, with chaos lurking. It needed to be squelched. Summoning all the majesty and power of his robes, he took a step forward. "As your priest, I order you to stop this very instant!" he boomed.

A groan escaped from Fausto, deep and despairing. His eyes rolled up in his head. The broom fell from his hand. He pitched to the pavement like a sparrow struck by a slingshot's pebble; while around the piazza in unison rose the bleating of fifty sheep, as if a chorus of ovine hallelujahs.

The Monsignore felt the first eruption of boils.

⁓

"NOT TO WORRY," said Father Tommaso to Don Federico later that morning, applying a poultice to the elder priest's back, a mixture of egg, nutmeg and soot from the chapel floor, a reliable cure for boils. "It's nothing. The ravings of a demented mind. It will soon be forgotten."

"You're sure of that?" said Don Federico.

"Nothing more than a nuisance," soothed Father Tommaso.

Three hours later, Morelli's horse threw a shoe. The next afternoon Poggio the tailor, digging a site for his new privy, unearthed a set of silver candlesticks buried by his great-grandmother decades before. That same evening the Widow Costa heard the mooing of her cow coming from her chimney. These things were small; no visitation of crows had blackened the noonday sky, no plague of rabbits sprang from the soil; the evening star shone bright as always. No matter: by the next afternoon the town of Monte Castella was abuzz with the astonishing rumor: Fausto the fool, lowborn jester, foul-smelling object of pity and ridicule and scorn, had spoken to God in the well. And God had spoken back.

"*Baggianate*. Bullshit," grumbled Nonno, sliding loaves from the bakery oven. "The bimbo heard the sound of his own farts."

"His prophecies came true," said Mamma.

"Dig long enough by anyone's outhouse, you're bound to dig up something," scoffed the old man. But Mamma crossed herself and said a Hail Mary.

It was baffling; to no one more than Fausto himself. For a man whose geography encompassed a single acre, whose days were measured by the number of stones he swept, whose sole possession was his broom, the sudden singling out by a Supreme Being who up to now had seemed comfortably distant was troublesome at best, terrifying at worst. The events of that certain morning, at least what he retained of them, seemed to have happened to someone else, in another place. It was all beyond his grasp. He could only hope that God, having had His say, was finished with him.

25

Alas, God was not. Three nights later, the voice again summoned Fausto, trembling, knees clattering, to the well.

"He practically floated across the square," reported Ernesto Capelli, the night concierge at the Grand Hotel Imperiale, to Don Federico the following morning.

"As if moved by invisible hands," added Carlotta Rampone, whose occupation often kept her late at the same hotel.

Don Federico surveyed the seemingly lifeless body on the cobblestones. For a moment he wondered wistfully if the application of the Last Rites might be required.

"Salvami, Signore!" croaked Fausto, his eyes flying open. *"Che Dio abbia pieta di noi."*

Don Federico's reservoir of patience was running low. "I order you to stop this imbecility now!" he barked. "Am I understood?"

Fausto eyed the nightshirt looming above him. "Attend thy step, lest thy feet become confused" he croaked, almost plaintively.

"I warn you," barked the Monsignore. "No more!" With that he spun on his heel and stalked way.

Seconds later he turned his ankle ascending the church steps, and had to be carried to his rooms.

<hr/>

BY WEEK'S END a change had come over Piazza Piccola. The well had begun to resemble a crude altar, bedecked with flowers, rosary beads and candles. Likewise was Fausto's shelter beside the church steps festooned with coins and personal icons as befitted the abode of a former nitwit now declared prophet. Carts and horses, even the occasional automobile slowed to a crawl as they passed, while at a respectable distance small groups kept watch on Fausto's hut, determined to witness first-hand his next conversation with God and with luck be rewarded with a glimpse into their own fortunes.

The unexpected attention wrought a change in Fausto. Sudden celebrity was like a warm blanket to a man who had lived his life in the cold. Where once people shunned him, now they stood - even knelt - in line to offer gifts, to touch his clothes. As for the voice that called from the well and the words that jumped from his tongue, who was he, a simple sweeper of stones, to say if it were prophecy or imagination?

"He's issuing marriage advice," groaned Don Federico as Father Tommaso piled on more poultice and wrapped his ankle in bandages.

"God is testing your patience," soothed Father Tommaso.

"The archbishop is due in ten days," wailed the Monsignore.

"There may be a solution," suggested Tommaso. "Invite Fausto back to Mass."

"Never!" cried Don Federico. Never would he consider giving in.

Thus it was that late that night, under cover of dark, a figure, limping slightly, moved down the church steps and softly, cautiously knocked at the entrance to Fausto's hut. Inside, bent double in the tiny space, Don Federico confronted his nemesis, who was at the moment warming, over a small flame, an excellent rabbit *rillette aux foie gras*, a gift from Signor Bellini, the chef at the Grand Hotel Imperiale, for whom Fausto had prophesied a hefty bequest from a distant and unnamed relative.

"*Vino, Monsignore?*" asked Fausto, pointing hospitably to a cache of bottles provided by Fanelli the wine merchant.

Don Federico had not come to sup. He put his cards on the table. "I've no wish to see this outrage continue, my son. As your Monsignore, I am charged with the protection of your soul. Do you not agree?"

Fausto only stirred his *rillette*. In the tiny space the aroma of foie gras was like heady perfume.

"Some say I should punish you for your acts of blasphemy," lied Don Federico. "However, given the circumstances, I might consider an exception. Assuming, of course, you will stop this masquerade."

Fausto stirred the pot. The Monsignore's stomach began to growl.

"What masquerade?" said Fausto.

"Surely," cried the priest, "you don't believe you actually talk to God?"

"But Monsignore," replied Fausto, once again feeling the swirl of logic wrap him like a coil. "It is God who talks to me. As you suggested. Remember? You said I should –"

"Never mind what I said!" roared Don Federico. The miasma of spices was making him dizzy; it occurred to him a glass of chianti might help clear his head. A thought, terrifying in its implications, had begun to form in his mind: that Fausto might be telling the truth.

But if that were so, if God had indeed anointed this ragged wretch, this very embodiment of disorder, on the very steps of his own demesne...

It struck Don Federico that God had never spoken to him.

He leapt up, knocking his head on the stones of the roof.

"Let me be clear," he said, summoning whatever dignity he still possessed. "If you insist on defying my offer, I shall be forced to take action. I shall speak to Rome. Tonight. I shall request an order of excommunication!"

The stirring ceased. In the darkness, Fausto's eyes widened.

"Do I make myself clear? No more prophecies. *Basta!*" Don Federico pushed his way out of the hut, reeling, but convinced that at long last, order had been restored. Surely no one, not even a fool, would risk the everlasting condemnation of the Holy Church. And, indeed, the next morning Fausto failed to appear at the well. By evening, the entrance to his shelter had been blocked with newspapers and stones. The next day, nothing was seen of him, nothing heard. That night, Don Federico slept the sleep of the righteous: the matter, at last, was at rest.

Until Friday.

On Friday the well went dry.

PEBBLES were dropped. A bucket was lowered; nothing was heard but the hollow clank of metal on stone. A small boy – Quindici, the stonecutter's son – was sent down on a rope, and returned empty handed. (Niccolò had volunteered but Mamma said no, to his great disappointment). Naturally, the news was received with consternation: never in the history of Monte Castella had the well at Piazza Piccola been without water. Through flood and famine, battle and drought, it had faithfully served. Now, overnight, it had ceased to produce.

A delegation approached the rectory.

"What do they want me to do?" said Don Federico to Father Tommaso in the rectory office.

"They think it's the work of God," explained Father Tommaso. "They want you to help."

This is what happens when you consort with false prophets, thought Don Federico. But at least the swallows had found their way home. "Shall I assume, then, they want me to say a mass?" he asked.

Father Tommaso shook his head. "They want you to speak to Fausto. They want <u>him</u> to talk to God."

That was the final straw. Don Federico locked himself in his rooms and refused to come out.

For the next three days, whether due to pride, confusion, stubbornness, or simple faith, the situation remained at an impasse: Fausto immured in his hut, Don Federico barricaded in his rooms. Then, on the fourth day, something notable happened.

On the fourth day, the well began to stink.

It was an odor unlike any known to a citizenry well-versed in the smell of barnyard and manure pit; a reek so strong that doors and windows were closed, even in the heat of summer. And with that stench, emanating outward in all directions from the well, the moment arrived for religion's bastard children to make their appearance. One in particular.

"*Malocchio!*" whispered Barzini the ice man.

"*Malocchio!*" nodded Boldini, the pharmacist.

"A curse," spat the Widow Petacci, thereby making the rumor fact. "The well has been cursed!"

Malocchio, the evil eye. Across the piazza the seeds of superstition, dormant up to now, blossomed like wildflowers in a gentle rain. Gestures were made, omens watched for; the devil's horn, worn to ward off evil spirits, made its appearance everywhere. At the *caffè*, on the streets, in haylofts and bedrooms, the issue was pondered. And, as always in matters of great community peril, blame was assigned. "Fausto. The fool has the Eye. Fausto's cursed the well."

Just like that the town turned against him.

In place of coins on the roof of his hut, cloves of garlic appeared; in place of gifts, salt was sprinkled at his door. Those who dared to pass close by made sure to spit over their shoulders. Plans were discussed to burn the hut and chase the malingerer out of town; all while, Fausto himself remained in his stone hovel, confused and frightened, cowering in dread.

As for Don Federico, the Monsignore of the Church of San Bartolomeo Giusto had seen his worst nightmare come to fruition. Despite his best efforts – perhaps because of them – chaos had triumphed. His once-orderly parish was drowning in apostasy, blasphemy, vengefulness and fear; all with the Archbishop due to arrive in a matter of days. Yet even still he held on to his principles. He thought of his mother, long departed, who raised him to keep the house clean, to sweep the floors, to order the spices and name the chickens.

She, too, was prone to boils.

That night Don Federico made his way down the center aisle of the church. Perhaps for the first time he looked at the portrait of St. Bartolomeo, holding in his hands a knife and the folds of his own flayed skin. Was it possible, thought Don Federico, that between order and chaos, God had left a tiny space?

At the altar he knelt. It wasn't the first time a man in robes had been brought to his knees by a man in rags. He reached to dip his fingers in the holy water.

It was then that God spoke to the priest.

That priest, however, was not Don Federico.

THE STORY of the midnight journey of young Father Tommaso into the hills above Monte Castella, riding his bicycle, guided by nothing more than a torch and the voice of God, was soon to become legend, at least to some.

How there, as if led by divine hand, the priest came upon a hidden ravine from which flowed an underground spring – as it happened, the long-searched for source of the well in the center of town far below. How, wedged into the spring, plugging its progress, lay the rotting corpse of a fallen cow belonging to Signora Costa the bricklayer's widow; how, with the strength of ten men, the young Tommaso cleared the blockage of fetid flesh and bone, thereby freeing the water to flow. And how, the following Sunday, the arrival of the Archbishop coincided with the Restoration of the Waters, as noted officially in Vatican History, though curiously not celebrated on Piazza Piccola, where few souls wished to remember it happened at all.

If, in fact, it did.

Soon other events, more immediate and profound than the voice of God, would conspire to render such a memory obsolete. In the coming chaos the Miracle of the Well, like the well itself, would become part of the rubble.

In the meantime, on the piazza, people occasionally left a coin on Fausto's shelter.

The Widow Costa purchased a new cow.

Don Federico requested permission to enter the Monastery at Monte Oliveto Maggiore, on account of his boils, but was refused.

Father Tommaso's bicycle resides to this day in the Vatican, though no one seems to know exactly where.

LA MAESTRA LEONORA

When the letter arrived informing Leonora and Renata Franchetti
of their uncle's death and of a bequest which he had left them, it
was decided that Renata should travel to Naples to meet the lawyer to sign
papers. Leonora would stay behind. It would be the first time they had been
separated since childhood.

They lived together on Via Venti Settembre, just two streets off Piazza
Piccola. So far as was known neither had had a suitor for many years,
although Renata had once been engaged and Leonora was considered by
many to be pretty. Their life together was organized and efficient, and

although they had occasional differences they had divided their household duties so neither one was inconvenienced. They had done this years ago and saw no reason to change.

Renata worked at the *farmacia* but Leonora taught school and couldn't leave her students; therefore Renata would go. She would travel by car to Pienza and from there by train to Naples. She would stay with relatives and be back in exactly two weeks. In preparation for the trip Renata, who did most of the cooking, prepared some soups and sauces for Leonora, plus sandwiches for the train, and set out a jigsaw puzzle for her sister to work on, though Leonora assured her she wouldn't have time.

With all that taken care of early on a Sunday morning the sisters bid goodbye with a hug and a fond wave. For Leonora the departure of her sister caused no great concerns. She wouldn't be lonely; she had friends in the community, was well thought of at the shops; had the company of her cat. She didn't mind solitude. Most of all, happily, she had her students.

The school where she taught was just up the hill from the piazza. Here in a sunlit classroom decorated with maps and artwork and shells from distant seas, along with the required portrait of *Il Duce* gesturing in the direction of the janitorial closet, Maestra Leonora – her title as teacher – watched over her flock of young students, including the boy Niccolò and his friends. It could be said that the *Maestra* brought to them a love of learning through her tender care, her passion for beauty, and her patient disregard for the flood of new regulations arriving daily from Rome. What did politicians know of poetry?

In return for her care her students showed a penchant for being inspired; especially the boys, who found in the Maestra's soft curves and commodious bottom a new and intriguing object of study. From her hour of rising to mid-afternoon, the welfare of her students – their antics, their hopes, their dilemmas – were Leonora's sole concern. It was only in the evening that her thoughts turned to other things, most often involving her sister. Now, with Renata absent, she suddenly found herself facing an odd, new feeling.

It wasn't loneliness. How could it be? She was a woman of ingenuity. She sewed, wrote in her diary, tended to her small garden in the yard, fed her cat, read books. So it wasn't loneliness. Nor was it regret for her life with Renata; long ago they had learned to put up with the title of spinster. It was more a sudden, vague sensation of something undone in her life, some destiny unmet, some gift ungiven or, perhaps, unreceived.

But these were not feelings Leonora dwelled upon. She had her classroom and that was enough. There, surrounded by manifestations of thought and beauty she felt in touch with the highest aspirations of man. Dante, Petrarch, Keats – she saw them as pure and unsullied, uncompromised by the unsettling events stirring outside her classroom window, both in Rome and very much closer.

Even the young man with the bloody face lying crumpled in the schoolyard was not, at first, enough to change that.

By the time Leonora had rushed from the classroom to chase his attackers away; by the time she'd helped him inside, her blouse was soaked in his blood. It was late afternoon, the infirmary staff had left, so she treated his wounds herself, wiping the broken tooth, dabbing the swollen eyelids, gently washing the cuts and bruises along his ribcage under his torn shirt, applying the bandages with gentle care. During this he sat moaning softly, dark hair matted, soaked with the spittle of his tormentors. When she had done what she could he once again became recognizable as a former student of hers, once a boy, now seventeen. "Vincenzo?" she said.

"Cowards," sneered Vincenzo Nutti. "They jumped me, then ran." But he knew she knew better and turned his swollen face away. It wasn't the first time the young man, who was not big, not handsome, nor gifted with grace, had been preyed upon in the yard. In the way that circumstance assigns each youth a particular role in the hierarchy of his contemporaries, to Vincenzo had fallen the role of whipping boy, object of contempt. Deserving or not he in turn had, perhaps unwittingly, molded himself to the part. His awkward bearing and unfashionable dress seemed to invite the taunts and humiliation of the other boys of the class, the strongest of whom had ascended to a new status as members of Mussolini's Vanguard Musketeers, whose fraternity defined the ideals of the strong, the fit, the black-shirted *popolare*.

"Someday they'll crawl before Vincenzo Nutti," he boasted now, in the safety of Maestra Leonora's gentle ministrations. And despite the fact that his empty bravado was vaguely obnoxious to her, her heart went out to him. And because it was after school, and she had time, and because her house was empty; perhaps even further because she was in no hurry to be alone, she invited him home for tea.

"Why?" he said "Because you pity me?"

"Not at all," replied Leonora, even though she did. "You certainly don't have to come."

But he came, walking behind her a step lest anyone think he was cleaving to her for protection; while Maestra Leonora, wondering whether to serve the boy biscotti or cakes, strode ahead, head erect, with a smile for everyone they passed, some of whom – the men – could not be blamed for a backward glance at her subtle pulchritude, the arch of her buttocks, the curve of her calves, though of course these were thoughts unbecoming of both her character and reputation. By the time they had reached Via Venti Settembre, Leonora had made up her mind. "It will be cakes," she thought.

"The boy will like those." When she unlocked the door to her apartment, however, he hesitated, a look of sullen distrust on his face. Leonora laughed.

"*Dai, entra!*" she said. "Don't be afraid. The world won't end. Perhaps you'll feel like talking."

Inside she motioned Vincenzo to wash his hands in the lavatory while she moved to the kitchen to start the kettle. She smiled as she noticed her sister had, before she left, sorted the teas into cannisters. So like Renata even if it was the slightest bit annoying. A thought began to form in her mind that should something go wrong with Renata's trip, should her train hop the tracks, that Leonora could go on living here quite at peace. But she quickly turned it away.

Then she noticed the cat outside the window, looking in, wide-eyed, but not at her.

The boy was on her before she had time to turn; she knew only the shock of his weight, his hands at her neck. His charge pushed them both to the floor, he clutching at her dress. Then the clatter of his belt buckle, hands pushing her thighs apart, her underthings ripping.

Had her sister been there, she would have cried out. Instead, she made herself very still, quiet, bracing for the pain. It never came. She noticed he was laboring. He rolled away and sat up. She looked up to see him sobbing.

Instinctively, she reached out to stroke his head.

THEY SAT at the kitchen table, having tea. "Are you going to tell?" he said.

"Is that what I should do?" she asked, not certain herself.

"If you tell." he said, "my father will whip me. If you tell I'll be ruined."

"Why did you do it?" she asked. He didn't respond.

"Was it because I was kind?" she said.

"No one is kind. People act like they do to get what they want. When they have it they're done with you. The world is a battleground. Be strong or be lost." He hung his head, afraid to meet her gaze.

"You have been listening to too many broadcasts," she said, and poured him more tea; the cakes had been ruined.

"It's because of the Yids," he said.

"I'm a Yid," said Leonora

"You're different," said Vincenzo.

"How is that?" she asked. But he had no reply.

Then she led him to the bedroom and they made love. She felt his pain, his anger, his shattered mouth, the shape of his ribs; now, the body she had ministered to was alive with hunger and rage. She shuddered and came.

Later when he had gone she wondered if what she had done was right. She knew it wasn't. She thought about writing her sister, but that would only have complicated Renata's journey. Besides, Renata would surely not approve; the young man was only seventeen.

What was odd was that she felt no shame. She was alive. She felt her sin alive inside her, only hers, belonging to no one else. She felt the poets would understand, might feel as she did.

She decided not to mention the matter at all.

THEY SAW EACH OTHER AGAIN, and again after that; in fact, nearly every afternoon after school. Now they walked the steps to her house apart; first Leonora then, lingering a block behind, Vincenzo, as if someone might be watching, though surely no one was. She was surprised by the *frisson* of excitement this masquerade caused in her: to be followed, as if stalked and hunted, then, once at home, possessed by his fury.

Afterwards, in bed or in the kitchen, Vincenzo talked; he couldn't stop. The more confident he became, the more his swagger returned, as if being with her infused him with an unpleasant strength, a bitterness she could not fathom in such a young man. His petty resentments, his fear of ridicule and rejection, his almost fanatic worship of *il Duce* seemed to her comical, or if not that, repulsive. Yet, he excited her, perhaps because she could touch him, fondle him; perhaps only because he was there.

At the shops people noticed a change. Leonora blushed, and blamed the weather. Mornings she found herself rising early, singing to herself over breakfast, while the cat watched in puzzlement from the windowsill. In the classroom, as she read the lessons, she was thinking of him.

A letter from Naples. Renata wrote that things had gone well with the lawyer: however, due to a persistent cough which, though not serious, continued to linger, she had decided to stay a week longer. Leonora, though concerned about her sister's health, could not deny a feeling of relief. Now there would be more time before...before what? She hadn't considered where all that had happened might lead. She had made it a point not to. How in the world could she ever explain to anyone, much less Renata?

"Dearest Sister," she wrote. "A cough is nothing to take lightly. For your own well-being, I urge you to stay until you've fully recovered. Though I miss your company, I am prepared to make do, for as long as it may require."

Having written the lie she posted it and went to bed. Tomorrow was school, then the week's end; she wasn't to see Vincenzo again until Monday.

OVER THE NEXT FEW DAYS the world and everything in it seemed to echo Leonora's secret bliss. The blue of the sky, the whisper of trees, music emanating from distant windows, all conspired to ratify her joy. Poems she had recited for years overflowed with new meaning. Her students puzzled at her unexpected laughter and giggled at her unexplained distraction.

On Monday, however, when Vincenzo did not appear to follow her, she walked home alone and carefully covered the cakes in the kitchen. Had something gone wrong? Was he alright? Was she mistaken about the day? Or something worse? She poured a bath and read a book, gently stroking the cat while all around, cracks and fissures appeared in the facade she had so carelessly constructed.

When Friday came and still no sign of Vincenzo she decided, against all her better judgment, to look for him. She found him in the piazza, by the statue of Garibaldi, among a crowd of young men, his hands in his pockets, slouched like the others, smoking a cigarette and talking. She had never seen him smoke before. She could see his talk had attracted the others' attention; they listened and smirked, as if hearing a dirty joke. She suspected the young men were the same ones who had beat him before.

He saw her. The others did, too. Immediately their eyes confirmed her fears. Their smirks contorted. One of them pointed and laughed; then the others. The mocking began. They grinned, spat on the stones, and dug their elbows into each other.

She kept her eyes on Vincenzo. His face had gone ashen, sickly. He motioned for her to go, but she couldn't move.

"That's enough," he said to the boys. "She doesn't deserve that. Leave her alone."

They turned on him. "Who the fuck are you," they sneered. "You piece of shit, think you're some kind of big deal because you fucked an old woman? *Imbecille.* You're bragging you fucked an old yid? Look at her! Probably gave you a dose of the clap, you maggot. *Verme!*"

Then, bored with the whole business, they stamped their cigarettes into the stones and walked away, one or two still laughing, others already done with the joke. Only Vincenzo remained, looking puny and frightened.

"Do you want to come to the house?" she said.

"Fuck you," he said. "Why did you come here?"

"I didn't know where you were. I thought you might be hurt."

"You've made a joke of me," cried Vincenzo. "It's your fault this happened. Now you've ruined my chances."

He turned and stalked across the piazza. She wanted to call after him, but her throat was stopped, and her lungs were empty.

THE WEATHER TURNED unexpectedly sultry, Leonora went about her business, taught her class, shopped for her groceries, straightened her house and read her books, as if the past three weeks had never happened. They had, of course, and she felt quite sure that people would hear, if they hadn't already. Then she would have to explain, though she could think of no explanation that would be satisfactory, or even true. Renata wrote that her cough had improved, she'd be home in just a few days, and that she had, she thought, some very good news. But Leonora knew that things between them would change once Renata knew, though they would probably never speak of it.

Then the following Wednesday Leonora returned home from school to find on her front porch her cat, hanging lifeless at the end of a rope. She buried it in her garden, went inside and sat at her kitchen table, her eyes on the kettle she'd fixed the day she brought the boy home. Evening came, lightning flashed; rain began to fall, a voluptuous summer storm. Leonora sat, untethered. In the gathering dark, she took off her clothes. She had never been naked outside her bedroom.

She went to the window; in the dark the rain poured down, sultry and cool. She opened the door and walked outside. The rain felt good on her body. She moved to the gate, pushed it open and stepped into the street.

The storm had arrived unexpectedly, violently, drenching the hot stones of Piazza Piccola with a sudden, cooling mist. Through the refracted light of the downpour people rushed for cover, heads bowed; in their hurry to find shelter, no one noticed her, or her nakedness. The mist swept around her feet like a cloud. She felt as if she were floating. It was as if she had become pure spirit, hovering clear of the pulse of the world. She started across the square. A baby cried from an opened upstairs window; shop bells tinkled in the wind; high atop the Grand Hotel Imperiale the flags snapped and barked like dark sentries. Lightning danced overhead; the thunder crackled across to the mountains, then turned and boomed softly back. Invisible, weightless, she moved past the well toward the row of shops huddling under a column of streetlights.

As she approached, in the brightly-lit window of the bakery a small boy's face peered through the raindrops, out to the circle of light on the pavement, just beyond which she hovered, naked and transformed. The boy's hand traced a raindrop's journey across the glass; then – had he seen? – his small hand reached up, as if in tentative signal. She backed away into the shadows. The rain fell harder.

Out of the dark loomed the church, impassive, sullen, doors closed against the weather. At the rectory next door, the Monsignore splashed in his bath, contemplating the symmetry of the psalms, while in the fetid shelter next to the steps the village fool slept curled in his nest of rags. Down the lane lay the schoolhouse, maternal, pregnant with hope. Everywhere was the life she knew, or had known, to which she could no longer return. The winds increased. The thing that had been alive in her slipped away, wings spread, carried into the night aloft on the storm. She found a bench, and sat. By now, the stones had given up their heat. Drenched and shivering, she felt heavy, and came back to earth; in despair, she wept.

With that, among the whirling spirals of mist one took shape and approached, as if a ghost, and seemed to sit next to her, and became a thing she could trust.

"Leonora," it said. "The poetry of the earth is never dead."

And this was true.

So rising, she made her way home and dried herself off and slept wrapped in blankets and did not dream, while outside her windows the columns of mist stood guard, sentries in the fog, lest anything of the flesh disturb her peace.

The next day there would be lessons to prepare. The day after that Renata would be home; Renata, who had had an adventure of her own in the city of Naples, and had met a man, and would soon be leaving Piazza Piccola to spend her life with him.

But the scandal Leonora expected never occurred. In a small town like Monte Castella there was a place for the fallen: forgiven but preserved, held in the town's knowing embrace like an insect in amber. Given that, it might be thought that Leonora went on, perhaps relieved to live alone, still reading the poets but knowing now there was cruelty, real and alive, in the world.

However, this was not the case.

The gift ungiven, it turned out, was money. The uncle's bequest made Renata and Leonora rich. By the time the darkest days came to Piazza Piccola Leonora had moved to London, to live out her years near Hampstead Heath.

Within view of the home of John Keats.

THE RUINS

Beyond the piazza, less than a quarter of a mile past the *cimitero*, past the stonemason's yard and the barn where Signora Costa, the bricklayer's widow, keeps her cows, lies a field of scattered stones; massive, silent, long ago fallen. Lovers go there to spoon, cats to mate, young boys to play at war and destruction. In summer, flowers grow in riot, as if to cover the shame of decrepitude with the shameless folly of youth.

These are the Roman ruins: crumbling walls, a tumbled archway, remnants of fluted columns, a set of granite stairs leading upward to nowhere. It pleases the town – when they bother to think of it at all – to imagine that once the place was considered worthy of a temple, though in fealty to which god or goddess is of some dispute. In general the ruins are simply tolerated, like grandparents in the home of busy children: on Piazza Piccola, people have more pressing concerns.

Perhaps the clairvoyant might guess at events that will transpire among those stones on a day not far removed: the stamping of boots, the barking of guns, the cries of lamentation. Or hear in advance the buzz of the airplanes, like vengeful wasps overhead. But no one guesses, and no one hears - least of all the ruins themselves, whose granite slumbers are long past disturbance by the mere caress of bombs.

For now, the flowers bloom.

IL BORSEGGIATORE

Let us imagine that Giuseppe Rosario Almonte began his life in Milan, the youngest of fourteen siblings whose father, Luigi Almonte, made a decent if not extravagant living as a *borseggiatore* – that is to say, a pickpocket. Let us further imagine that, wishing to carry on the family name, all fourteen of Luigi's sons and daughters chose to follow in their revered father's footsteps. This flood of light-fingered Almontes onto the local market inevitably resulted in a glut, forcing the younger siblings ever outward in search of more fertile territories. By the time Giuseppe – youngest and by far most talented of the clan – was ready to assume his station, not only Milan, but most of the towns and cities around, had been picked clean. Hardly a street corner, train station or crowded nightclub remained where a gifted young fingersmith might ply his trade.

So at the age of fifteen Giuseppe, like a young lion, set off across Italy in search of unspoiled territory in which to practice his craft. After many adventures and misadventures, he stumbled upon what he was looking for: an insignificant piazza on the outskirts of a no less insignificant town. Here, the young man sensed a canvas on which to paint his masterpiece. Here, he chose to plant his flag.

And here, on Piazza Santa Caterina Piccola, Giuseppe Almonte flourished.

His talents at the art of legerdemain, as mentioned, were prodigious. The young man, it would seem, was born to relieve others of their possessions. His hands were like *ali d'angelo* – the wings of an angel. He never missed a mark and was never caught, nor even accused, though many had their suspicions. And although the local population was hardly dripping with wealth, between the occasional guest at the Grand Hotel Imperiale and the late night crowd of drunks at the *caffè*, Giuseppe gleaned enough to keep himself more than comfortable. When cash was required, he simply strolled down the Via Venti Settembre in the evening, mixed with the evening *passeggiata*, filched a wallet or lifted a watch, *senza problemi*. All in all, life for Giuseppe Almonte was comfortable.

Perhaps, for an artist, too comfortable.

Over time, as with any finely skilled artisan at the peak of his powers, Giuseppe began to look for new challenges. Like Paderewski playing scales, the simple picking of pockets had become child's play. So, to scratch his itch and keep his interest from flagging, Giuseppe began to set himself obstacles to overcome. For a time he limited himself to lifting only diamond rings; then amethyst; then only necklaces; then only those with natural pearls.

When that grew stale, he moved to spectacles, buttons, and barrettes, and after that, cufflinks and bowties. But despite these challenges he continued to be bored.

He filched musical instruments out from under their owners' gaze: violins, trumpets, once even a bass drum – though, it being the only bass drum on Piazza Piccola, he surreptitiously returned it in time for the annual San Gennaro parade, after which he stole it again. He tried working blindfolded; then walking backwards; then with gloves on. He made off with the Mayor's shoelaces, and when the Police Chief came to investigate, Giuseppe lifted the Police Chief's toupee. The next night, he put them all back.

He purloined the Widow Petacci's corset in broad daylight.

Yet even these reckless diversions seemed to Giuseppe no more than parlor tricks. A terrible thought began to haunt him: perhaps at his young age he had reached a dead end. There was nothing, it seemed, he couldn't steal; worse, there was nothing to steal which he had not already stolen at least once before. Perhaps he was doomed to spend the rest of his life simply repeating the past.

Then, one evening, purely by accident, he stumbled upon the grail he had been seeking. Like so many other things of great value in life, it was found in the eyes of a beautiful girl.

She sat alone, weeping into her napkin, at Menucci's outdoor *caffè*, on a night lit with stars and the sparks from Menucci's smoke pots, meant to mask the smell of the stables next door. Nearby sat Giuseppe Almonte, sipping a glass of fine chianti compliments of an overstuffed businessman who, somewhere across town, was just now realizing that his wallet, not to mention his tie clip, were missing. Giuseppe watched as the young woman dabbed her eyes. Even from a distance, her grief was palpable, almost as if it had heft and volume. As to the nature of the grief, there was no telling. Loss, betrayal, infidelity, disappointment, death; whatever the cause, it clung to her like an amulet of sorrow.

At least, so it seemed to Giuseppe.

The napkin slipped from her lap; in a flash, he was on his feet, stooping to grab the napkin almost before it drifted onto the pavement. "*Permette, signorina. Il vostro tovagliolo,*" he smiled.

She turned. He handed her the napkin; and, in that moment, with a single, deft swipe of his hand, lifted from her the strands of her terrible grief.

And this was the remarkable thing: by the time the young woman had replaced the napkin on her lap, her tears had already begun to dry. Her sighs diminished; her absent smile returned. Reaching for her wine, as if suddenly reawakening to her surroundings, it occurred to her to thank the gentleman who had handed her the napkin.

But by then, like all good thieves, he had left the scene, in possession of treasure no *borseggiatore* in all of history had ever before possessed.

LET US NOW imagine that, having plucked a thing as insubstantial as a young woman's grief out from beneath her very eyes, Giuseppe might have been content to rest on his laurels and return to the getting of cash. After all, what was grief worth on the open market? Certainly the supply of sorrow in the world was well overstocked; no competent fence would touch it. And yet, there was something in the feel of it: a smooth and liquid evanescence that drew Giuseppe to it and made it treasure. That very evening Giuseppe acquired – from the luggage of a Polish countess travelling by limousine into exile in Firenze – a jewelry box made of ivory, lined with silk and inset with diamonds and rubies. In this he set his prize and went to bed. And when that night Giuseppe dreamt, great vistas opened before him. Like Columbus on the coast of Spain, a new world, unimagined by previous generations of Almontes, beckoned.

The next day Giuseppe set sail.

That afternoon he made off with an old man's regrets; a night later, a young tough's braggadocio. On Sunday a single hour at Mass netted him a wife's despair, a young boy's shame and a lawyer's hypocrisy (though the lawyer, it turned out, had more where that came from).

A coward's fear, a miser's greed, a gossip's spite; one afternoon, on the Via Venti Settembre, Giuseppe plucked the bitterness from the mouths of an angry father and son. One by one these treasures found their way into the box by Giuseppe's bed.

Some things, he found, were harder to steal than others: patience and hope clung to their owners like nettles; valor was inseparable from its host; and when it came to virginity, Giuseppe left well enough alone. Even so, as weeks passed, the box at his bedside began to fill.

Until one afternoon when he returned to his apartment to find an invitation slipped under the door.

⌒

THE NAME OF THE GENTLEMAN awaiting him in the sumptuous dining room of the Grand Hotel Imperiale was Don Roberto Schivelli, *un uomo d'onore* – man of respect – who had travelled to Monte Castella from the south, perhaps from as far away as Sicily. The roughness of his complexion was matched by the perfection of his fingernails. Instantly

Giuseppe recognized the man's name and title, and admired his suit, on which the gleaming buttons were pearl.

"*Maestro*," began the Don when Giuseppe had been seated. "I have come to pay my respects. Word has reached me of your accomplishments."

"*Con tutto il rispetto*," replied Giuseppe, "I fear your journey has been in vain. I have no accomplishments to speak of."

"Of course," smiled Don Roberto, the wrinkles around his eyes replete with the shadows of a hundred deaths. "Be that as it may, since I have journeyed this far, perhaps you might consider indulging an old man a favor." And although these words wore the cloak of request, it was clear that hidden beneath the cloak was a dagger of ultimatum.

"Whatever may be in my power," replied Giuseppe, adjusting his napkin.

Don Roberto poured the wine and leaned back. "I have had in my life a great deal of success, much of it wrenched from the bones and teeth of my enemies. Now, near the end of that life, I find myself laden with wealth and influence. But something else as well."

He eyed Giuseppe. "I am speaking of my sins." he said.

"Ah," said Giuseppe.

"They chafe. They itch. At night they make a noise like a howling wolf. Can you relieve me of them?"

"For that you would need a priest," said Giuseppe.

"I'd prefer to leave the Church out of it," replied the Don. "I have been known to have enemies there. Besides, the Church is for worship, not for the conducting of business." He smiled again. "Do this and I will make you rich."

"I have no need of money," said Giuseppe. "Besides, if you seek absolution –"

"I do not seek absolution." said the *Padrino*. "Only relief."

Still, Giuseppe hesitated. Don Roberto leaned forward.

"Try," he said, "I urge you." His eyes fell on Giuseppe's hands. "Such hands. I have heard them compared to *ali d'angelo*. The wings of an angel! What a shame it would be to see them made idle."

A moment passed.

"On the contrary," said Giuseppe, at which Don Roberto noticed his cufflinks had disappeared, after which it occurred to him his pearl buttons were gone. The color rose in his face.

"Enough with the parlor tricks," he growled. "Will you do this, or not?"

Giuseppe rose from his chair. "What makes you think I haven't?" he asked. He bowed and left.

That night Giuseppe dropped the *Padrino's* sins into the ivory box by his bed and paused to admire them. Next to the other treasures the sins looked wretched, gnarled, deformed. Despite this, or perhaps because of this, Giuseppe felt a sudden fondness for them. Content with his day's work, he slept.

Across the piazza, however, Don Roberto did not. Through the long night the *Padrino* thrashed and moaned, besieged with nightmares, taunted by specters of humiliation, impotence, and castration. For what is a man like Don Roberto without his sins?

By morning a second invitation had found its way under Giuseppe's door.

"I want them back," said the haggard Don that night at his sumptuous table. "I will pay any price."

The trouble was that Giuseppe had, by this time, become attached to the small, misshapen things, and was loathe to see them returned.

"Perhaps just the cufflinks and pearls –" he suggested.

"Fuck the cufflinks and pearls," spat the Don. "You have my sins. I want them back."

For a moment, Giuseppe considered his options, though perhaps he should not have.

"The problem is," he lied, "I sold them last night to a fence, a man I do not know, who took them away and did not tell me where."

"Find him," said the *Padrino*.

"And if I cannot?" said Giuseppe.

"I urge you to do so," said Don Roberto. "A man without his sins is like a pickpocket without his hands."

And though his words were unmistakable, at first Giuseppe refused to accept their meaning. Surely, he imagined, a man of his gifts need not be dictated to by a common thug. Such is the hubris, and the fallacy, of the artist.

Still, hours later, in the moonlit quiet of his apartments, the thought occurred that perhaps his achievements had, in fact, reached a culmination. Having dared to trespass upon the Lord's own dominion, where to go from there? Perhaps the moment had come to effect a final sleight-of-hand, a masterpiece, *a tour de force*.

So he did.

By morning, Giuseppe Almonte was gone from Piazza Piccola. No one saw him leave. Nor did a trace remain of the hundreds of earrings, purses and amulets he had stolen. Like a wallet from a rich man's vest, all of it simply disappeared. Along with it all went Giuseppe and his jewel-encrusted ivory box. Just like that. *Nel nulla*. Into thin air.

RUMORS surfaced. Some reported Giuseppe living in Naples, Peking or New York. Some reported him king of a small nation in Africa. Some reported him wealthy, some dead. None could be confirmed.

Let us imagine, however, that several years later, following a period of worldwide conflagration, a young man who had spent time on Piazza Piccola found himself, for reasons not germane to this story, traversing a bustling street in the ancient city of Tunis. There, in a shadowed doorway, he happened to spot a seated figure of such wretchedness that, at first, the young man recoiled in disgust. The figure, however, beckoned to him – not with his hands, but with his eyes, from which radiated an almost hypnotic power.

Drawn against his will the young wanderer stepped forward. In the shadows, the stench was overwhelming; rats and scarabs rustled among the stones.

"Well?" boomed the young man, loudly, to allay his sense of unease. "What have you got for me?"

The wretch spoke, almost inaudibly. "*Un Tesoro*," he croaked. "A treasure. *Unico*. More precious than black opal or gold."

The young man doubted this, given the state of the fellow's attire, which consisted of nothing more than a moth-eaten beggar's robe. Nevertheless, held in place by the stranger's eyes, he felt a compulsion to know more. "Let me see," he said.

The wretch nodded and, with a quick movement beneath the tattered cloak, pushed forward a box made of ivory, now chipped and cracked, clearly once encrusted with jewels, though those had for some time been lost or stolen, or sold.

"How much will you give me?" said the wretch.

"The box," said the young man, somewhat disappointed, "is worth very little."

The wretch shook his head, with a sigh of ineffable sadness. "And sin?" he said. "What of sin?"

From beneath his cloak he reached out to open the lid - not with his hands, for he had no hands. Instead, from the end of his arms extended two battered hooks. With these he grasped the lid and pulled it open. The young man looked in, then drew back in horror.

"What are they?" he cried.

The wretch smiled. When he spoke, in his voice rang a deep and indomitable pride.

"*Ali d'angelo,*" he boasted.

L'ACCOMPAGNATRICE

It has been said that genius, like bedbugs, can be found in the least likely places. It follows, then, that Piazza Santa Caterina Piccola had both. But while the bedbugs far outnumbered the beds, despite unceasing applications of starch, garlic and prayer, genius – true genius – was a great deal more rare. Nevertheless it did exist, hiding, as genius often does, in plain sight: in this case on the stage of the recently renamed *Cinema Duce*, formerly known as the *Teatro Buffone* (an irony not lost upon the less politically enchanted in town).

Here, three nights a week, when the house lights dimmed and the projector clattered to life, the mundane cares of the world were swept aside by the epic themes of life, death and love, unfolding before an audience whose lives were anything but epic. Farmer, merchant, barber, stonecutter sat in thrall to the doings of glamorous stars whose godlike existence in distant Rome or Hollywood could scarcely be imagined: Garbo, Valentino, Fairbanks, Pickford, Chaplin. Larger than life and a great deal more beautiful, they filled the screen with their lives of romance and derring-do. Their costumes were eye-popping, the settings sublime. And, of course – these still being the days of silent films in small towns such as Monte Castella – there was one other element, perhaps the most important of all.

La musica.

Which, in this case derived from neither Heaven nor Hollywood but from the stage of the theater itself where night after night an improbable female figure, festooned in glittering gown, ancient fox fur, flashing bracelets, velvet slippers and rhinestone tiara, sat at an upright piano, her eyes upturned to the screen, arms pistoning, hands flying as she coaxed from the keys an unerring accompaniment of humor, romance and grandeur.

Her name was Isobel Andoloro. She used no printed score; she played by ear, her melodies her own. And what melodies! Her rolling cadenzas underscored the breathless sweep of Valentino's scimitar; her arpeggios punctuated Chaplin's whimsical walk; no matter what the setting or who the star, her music never failed to stir the spirit, rend the heart, tickle the funnybone or set pulses racing.

Not that anyone noticed. Indeed, such was the skill of this curious prodigy that as she played, the audience, eyes fixed on the screen, heard her without hearing, laughed without thinking, thrilled without knowing why. For though on Piazza Piccola it was Isabel Andoloro who made the movies come alive, the fact was almost nobody knew it. Not that it mattered to Isobel. She wasn't in it for the applause.

She simply played what she saw.

As to a private life, she had none: no children, no lovers, no livestock, nor even friends. Weekends, from the moment she rose in the morning in her apartment across from the schoolyard, her thoughts were of the night's coming task. As evening approached she dressed for the occasion, and although she could hardly be said to be pretty – charitably she might be called ungainly – she dressed as she aspired, in the style of the latest movie-star magazines. A touch of lipstick and rouge served, in her mind, to feature her eyes, which she considered her most attractive asset. Add to that the aforementioned fox stole and tiara and the effect was distinctive, if not always wholly successful. It hardly mattered: in the dark no one could see her anyway.

Then at night, as the white pillar of light cut through the miasma of cigarette smoke and perfume to explode in glorious images upon the screen, it was Isobel's genius that gave those images a voice, painted their moods, endowed them with life, humor, and depth. Her eyes on the screen, she poured out her essence. She gave her heart. She played what she saw. But when the movie had ended, as the audience spilled out through the lobby beneath the glaring portrait of Benito Mussolini on one side and the luscious cleavage of Mae West on the other, did anyone think to acknowledge the work of the theater accompanist?

"*Mi sono commossa.* What acting!" Mamma would sniffle, dabbing her eyes.

"*Incredibile!*" Biggio the barber would marvel, while Ignacci the hotel maître d' shook his head in wonder. "The scenery – "*Magnifico!*""

Isobel's genius had made her invisible. Even when unexpected things started to occur.

⌒

IT BEGAN WITH "Dracula," starring Hungarian actor Bela Lugosi as the sinister Vampire Count of Transylvania. On opening night at the *Duce*, the audience huddled in fear as, cape swirling, the rapacious fiend advanced on his victim, Lucy Weston, played by the vulnerable Francis Dade. Overcome, Lucy swooned; whereupon Dracula, lust in his eyes, opened his jaws to reveal his gleaming, hideous fangs. It was a moment of pure terror.

Or it might have been. Instead, unexpectedly, the audience tittered. In place of gasps, there were giggles; which soon became chortles; then outright laughter, engulfing the crowd in a contagion of giddiness which continued, scene after scene, as the hapless Count, now exposed as no more than a hungry party-crasher, applied his fangs to neck after neck, each time inducing further gales of laughter. By the end of the film - the leering buffoon asleep in his coffin – all agreed the film had been a comic success, Lugosi a genius of satire.

As always, no one had paid attention to the music.

The following week, it was Charlie Chaplin's turn. The movie this time was "The Gold Rush," starring Chaplin as a down-on-his-luck Alaskan prospector sharing his cabin with a half-starved brute named Big Jim. In the opening minutes, when the Little Tramp boiled his own boot and served it to Big Jim for dinner, the audience roared. The boot was funny, Chaplin's reactions sublime.

Then things took a sinister turn.

When Big Jim began to imagine his puny cabin-mate as a delicious roast chicken, in the audience concern replaced amusement. In place of laughter came gasps of fear. Shouts went up from the balcony: "*Attento, vagabondo!*" Husbands shielded their spouses' eyes. It seemed a dark drama of death and cannibalism was about to unfold. Fortunately, at that moment, a bear barged into the cabin, diverting Big Jim's attention and sparing the little Tramp's life. But Chaplin's performance had been riveting; after the show no one doubted "The Gold Rush" was a drama of the highest degree.

No one but Signor Emilio Sassi, who managed the theater; indeed, whose father had managed it before him, in the days of vaudeville and variety, prior to which the address had been the site of a pig farmer's manure pile. Though not a student of music, Emilio had grown up with the movies and knew when things were, to put it mildly, amiss. He made up his mind to speak to Isobel; which, the following evening he did, as she took her seat and adjusted her tiara.

"Signorina Andoloro," called Emilio from the foot of the stage. "Is everything all right?"

Isobel, surprised to be noticed at all, turned and raised a penciled eyebrow.

"*Scusi?*" said Isobel.

"The music," Emilio ventured. "Chaplin was frightful last week. The week before the vampire had them rolling in the aisles."

"What vampire?" inquired Isobel.

"Dracula," replied Emilio.

"Oh," said Isobel, flexing her fingers.

"Did you mean to –"

"I play what I see," said Isobel. "Has someone complained?"

Emilio had to admit no one had.

"Well then," said Isobel. With the issue resolved, at least in her mind, she turned to the keyboard and launched into a medley of *il Duce*'s favorite songs, among them *Giovinezza* and "I've Got A Lovely Bunch of Coconuts," which the powers in Rome had ordered performed at the beginning of every performance, like it or not.

And although his discussion with Isobel had been less than conclusive, and although he couldn't help noticing that her lipstick had been somewhat carelessly applied, much of it well to one side of her mouth, Emilio decided to leave matters at that. The fact was, no one *had* complained; in fact, the audiences seemed pleased. Perhaps, he decided, it was best to let the pianist play.

A week later, it happened again.

The film this time was "Keystone Hotel," starring the feckless Keystone Cops. Ordinarily these benighted, bowl-hatted policemen provoked gales of laughter as they waved their batons, leapt in the air, and tumbled over each other in calamitous pratfalls. This night, however, perhaps swayed by a *rallentando* of noble chords from the piano, the audience broke into spontaneous applause, overcome with appreciation for those noble, unsung, heroic underdogs of law enforcement.

Witnessing this, Emilio felt a growing sense of unease.

"What have you done to the Keystone Cops?" he called to Isobel, catching up to her as she left the stage.

"Who?" said Isobel.

This time Emilio would not be put off. "As I have learned from experience, funny is funny," he said. "And sad is sad."

"Truth is beauty and beauty is truth," replied Isobel.

"Not in the movies," explained Emilio.

"There's no need to shout," said Isobel.

"I am simply requesting," continued Emilio in a more reasonable tone, "that you play what the film requires."

"I play what I see," replied Isobel. "Has someone complained?"

And indeed once again no one had. The audience, Emilio had to admit, seemed more pleased than ever.

"In that case," sniffed Isobel, "I will take my leave." Whereupon, she opened the door to the janitorial closet.

"That way," suggested Emilio, pointing.

"Of course," said Isobel.

"By any chance," said Emilio, "is there something wrong with your eyes?"

"My eyes," retorted Isobel, fixing him with a steady gaze, "are my most attractive asset." With that she reached for the door, opened it, and left.

Which even then might have been enough for Emilio were it not for the fact that her steady gaze had been directed several feet over his head.

STILL, NO ONE <u>had</u> complained. Perhaps for this reason, not to mention the lack of suitable replacement pianists in a town the size of Monte Castella, Emilio Sassi once again swallowed his doubts, and Isobel Andoloro continued as accompanist at the *Cinema Duce*. As the weeks went on, however, it became clear that the music emanating from the stage no longer bore any connection to what was occurring onscreen. Whole sections of movies were being altered, plotlines reversed, characters reimagined. Ben Hur was a sissy, Buster Keaton a bully, Frankenstein's monster an irresistible master of sophisticated charm. Again, the audience failed to notice; accustomed as they were to letting the music speak, no one thought to question it. As a result, the moviegoers at the *Cinema Duce* became exclusive witnesses to stories and characters no one else in the world had seen: Chaplin, the tragic Tramp; James Cagney, the goofy Public enemy; the "It Girl," Clara Bow, with her eerily sinister and untrustworthy smiles. The delighted audience continued to grow with each week, filling the balcony and overflowing the orchestra. Business had never been better for Emilio Sassi. But, as with all things in the movies, it came at a price.

"You're going blind, aren't you?" called Emilio, late one night, watching Isobel stumble off the stage.

"What makes you say that?" said Isobel, her tiara sitting backwards on her head.

"Shall we stop this charade?" suggested Emilio. "It's clear you can't see."

"I see what I need to," replied Isobel.

"Nevertheless," said Emilio. "I can't have a blind pianist accompanying my movies, can I?"

"Has someone complained?" she asked, feeling her way past the janitor's closet and out the door.

"I demand an answer!" cried Emilio, who this time would not be put off.

On the curb, Isobel paused. "Beethoven was deaf," she intoned.

"Beethoven" said Emilio almost sadly, "never performed at the *Cinema Duce*! How can you play what you can't see?"

And although it was summer, and quite warm, even sweltering, Isobel pulled her fox fur tighter.

"How can I not?" she said, proudly raising her head. "If you don't like my work, find someone else."

"In the dark," said Emilio "no one will know you're gone."

"You might be surprised." Isobel said, and stumbled off the curb.

Left with no choice, Emilio did what he had to.

MAESTRO ALESSANDRO BRONZINO, noted accompanist from Campobasso, checked into the Grand Hotel Imperiale three days later, along with a steamer trunk bursting with popular sheet-music tunes. His impressive resume included engagements at the most prestigious movie houses in Rome and Milan, and though he did not play by ear, he did at least perform in a tailored tuxedo – *senza* tiara. Over the following weeks the estimable Maestro Bronzino took his place on the stage of the *Duce*, providing music for such films as "The Passion of Joan of Arc" starring Maria Falconetti and *La Bellezza Del Mondo* with Vittorio De Sica. His accompaniments lived up to his reputation: not a beat was missed, not a scene out of place. Funny was funny, and sad was sad. Musically speaking, things were what they should be. Emilio, needless to say, was pleased.

But people stopped coming.

At first, there were just a few empty seats, but by the third week, the balcony was bare. A week after that, even the orchestra was peppered with unoccupied spots. The situation could no longer be ignored. Emilio, concerned, stationed himself in the lobby, between Mussolini and Mae West, to eavesdrop as the audience – what there was of it – left the theater. What he found was this: something was missing, though nobody could say exactly what. Funny was funny, they said, and sad was sad. "*E allora?*" So what? They were bored. Of course, no one mentioned Isobel. No one had noticed she was gone, if they'd ever known she was there in the first place.

"Movies aren't what they used to be," yawned the last customer out. And the next night, no one came at all. Emilio ordered the projector shut down.

The following morning, unshaven, unable to sleep, Emilio knocked on Isobel's door. Isobel, dressed in tiara and furs, answered.

"What took you so long?" she inquired.

Emilio offered his arm.

"*Ars longa, vita brevis*," she said, and took it.

SO BEGAN what some recall as the Golden Age of Cinema on Piazza Santa Caterina Piccola. Unremarked upon by the world outside, the stage of the *Duce* witnessed an outpouring of creativity never dreamed of by the moguls of Hollywood or Rome. Three nights a week an audience of farmers, merchants, and stonecutters sat in thrall to an outpouring of genius unique in the universe – unpredictable, haunting, comical, tragic, sophisticated yet stirring. Responding to the shapes that flashed before her myopic eyes, Isobel's genius bloomed. Freed from the constraints of plot, character, and action, she played what she saw; or at least, what she thought she saw. And perhaps, near the end, even the audience who had ignored her began to understand the gift they had been bequeathed.

They kept coming. And Isobel played on, defiantly casting her music into the smoky night until, as in a Bette Davis tragedy, the darkness closed around her and even the shadows failed and she could no longer see. Even so, it wasn't her blindness that finally stopped her.

It was the talkies.

WHEN IN TIME the mighty film scores of such composers as Franz Waxman and Nino Rota filled movie houses with tidal waves of orchestral majesty, the role of *accompagnatrice musicale* was abandoned, an artifact of history, never quite noticed and hardly missed.

Except on Piazza Piccola. Here, people wondered whether "Gone with the Wind" might have been a superior film had the music been, not by Max Steiner of Hollywood, but by Isobel Andoloro on the stage of the old *Cinema Duce*. And although some of the younger crowd were embarrassed later in life to discover that Chaplin was in fact a comedian, while Lon Chaney was not, it only served to burnish Isobel's legend, such as it was, which – Piazza Piccola being quite small – was not very much.

Even so years later, in her apartment across from the schoolyard, Isobel continued to play on, unseeing and unseen, accompanying the tales of her own antic muse while in the schoolyard below, children stopped to listen, and jumped and whirled and danced. Indeed, even later, when the schoolchildren were gone, soldiers who were not very much older sat in the rubble, drinking from their helmets, weary of killing, and heard the music and dreamed of home.

LIBERTY

In winter, when the cold rains marched down from the mountains and swept across the piazza, the room Niccolò slept in was always warm. Directly below lay *il forno*, the oven, the heart of the bakery. There had been a time when the oven frightened the boy, like some great beast on cast iron feet, eyes flashing with fire. Now he was older, almost nine, and the beast had been tamed. He loved to watch his grandfather reach in with the peel to lift out the loaves, newly risen, sanctified, in a state of warm and tumescent grace. To Niccolò the bread smelled like Mamma. And Mamma meant home.

After school, as he raced in from the chill, there were muffins, *cannoli* and *bomboloni* beckoning from the shelves. And Mamma in her apron, discussing events of the moment with customers, shaking her head, pursing her lips, but saving her special look - eyes sparkling - for only him. Once a week like clockwork came the letter from America, rumpled and wafer-thin, seemingly breathless from its daredevil crossing of the sea. When it arrived, Mamma would put it in her apron and sing all day. Then at night, in the bed they shared, Mamma read aloud to Niccolò.

Papà wrote about life in the city of New York, where everything moved very fast. He worked cutting stone with a crew of men, some of them fools, some rascals, some honest, some not so honest. Soon, however, the job he'd been promised would come through; then Papà would be a baker in America and would send for Mamma and of course, Niccolò. Only Nonno would stay behind – he hated ships.

But this place, America: it was hard to hold in his mind. In Niccolò's world everything that was had always been, and would be: the bakery, the school, the church, his friends. Was there a piazza in America? Did the vegetable seller and his horse drowse there on summer afternoons? Did Fausto the fool sweep the stones? Was there a school, up the hill, in the nurturing shade of the olive trees? Who baked the bread in the oven, if not Nonno? In Niccolò's world all that changed were the seasons, and even they came back to where they began. At least they always had.

Now unsettling questions had begun to arise in this Eden of constancy. Around town posters appeared emblazoned with boastful phrases and clenched fists. At night Mamma and Nonno sat by the radio out of which sprang voices like hungry wolves, until Mamma wrung her hands and Nonno spat in the corner. More troubling still - at least, to a boy of nine - was a matter previously unknown and unimagined, a dark impenetrable mystery the clues to which, on Piazza Piccola, seemed impossible to come by.

<hr>

"Le melodie ascoltate sono dolci, ma più dolci ancora son quelle inascoltate." Poetry book in hand, Maestra Leonora turned to the window. As she did, a rubber band, launched from the bench behind Niccolò, snapped through the air and bounced off her well-girdled bottom. Maestra Leonora, communing with the poets, seemed not to notice. Around the room, three more rubber bands took wing, found their target, and bounced, each time without the slightest flinch from the Maestra.

"What did I tell you?" whispered Rinaldo, the ringleader of the assault, leaning forward to Niccolò and Quindici. "She's a virgin. Virgins don't feel a thing."

For Niccolò this was new information.

Rinaldo, who was older and therefore knew more, sat back on his bench, exchanging smirks with his conspirators around the room. But it didn't seem right to Niccolò to think of the Maestra that way. Next to Mamma, Leonora was the kindest woman he knew. As to the topic of her virginity...

"What's a virgin?" he asked Quindici, after school.

Quindici scoffed. "You don't know?"

"Exactly, I mean," said Niccolò.

Quindici eyed the sky and screwed up his face. Which meant Quindici didn't know, either.

Neither one of them knew, exactly, and this was a problem. In the cauldron of primary school, to be uninformed was to invite humiliation. There was, of course, the Virgin Mary herself, but what the mother of Christ had to do with Maestra Leonora's bottom was far from apparent. Besides, it was clear in the way the older boys talked that something profound – dark, yet tantalizing – lay hidden beneath their smirks: a code, impenetrable without the key, having nothing to do with church.

"Ouch!" cried Mamma that evening, turning from the stove, seeing the rubber band on the floor. "Niccolò, *cosa fai?*"

"*Niente, scusa,*" said Niccolò.

Frowning, Mamma turned away, rubbing her backside and muttering to herself. Clearly, she was not about to shed light on the matter, which was now even more perplexing; for although Mamma was slimmer and, of course, prettier than the Maestra, in most respects they seemed quite the same.

"Maybe you could ask your father," said Niccolò, since his own was not available, but Quindici shook his head. So, after more discussion and very nearly a fistfight they confronted Nonno in the bakery storeroom: Nonno, who had been a child in the days of Garibaldi and surely would know.

Nonno's grey eyes narrowed. "Why do you want to know?"

"It's important," replied the boys.

Nonno thought this over. "Do you know the bull?" he said.

"*Sì*" responded the boys.

"The bull has a pizzle," said Nonno.

"*Sì.*"

"Puts the pizzle in the heifer."

"*Sì.*"

"No pizzle, no calf." Nonno shrugged and spat. Having covered the subject, he went back to work.

They decided to try the priest.

"Bless me father, for I have sinned," said Niccolò in the confessional that afternoon.

"Make a good confession," said Don Federico.

"*Scusi, Padre*," piped up Quindici, who had crammed himself into the booth next to Niccolò. "We need to know what's a virgin."

There was silence behind the screen.

"How many are you?" said Don Federico

"It's important," chimed the two friends. "*Importante*."

Another silence, this one longer.

"The Virgin Mary," said Don Federico, solemnly, "was the mother of Jesus."

He waited, hearing whispers across the screen.

"But Monsignore," said Quindici, "Did the pizzle go in, or not?"

Wisdom comes at a price; ignorance can cost even more. For their blasphemies the boys received a penance of one thousand Hail Marys, plus the task of sweeping out church pews for a month. Quindici took a beating from his father's belt while Niccolò, at Mamma's behest, was subject to another of Nonno's explanations, more detailed than the first, but no less baffling as to the mysteries of Mamma, Mary and the schoolteacher's bottom, and why virgins have babies, if in fact they do, but heifers do not.

Things had reached an impasse. Perhaps, Niccolò reasoned, it might be best to remain patient and let matters sort themselves out. Sooner or later, an answer was bound to appear.

Which it did. In a manner of speaking.

ON HIS BIRTHDAY A PACKAGE arrived from New York. "A gift for my son, from the land of Liberty." Eight inches tall, made of copper, one hand holding the tablet of the law, the other upraised to brandish the flaming torch; her gaze, steadfast, determined. How brightly she shone as Niccolò unwrapped her. The Statue of Liberty! It must have cost Papà nearly half a week's pay.

"She stands for the most precious gift of all. Freedom." Papà wrote. "Take care of her, *mio figlio*." Instantly, Niccolò promised himself he would, no matter what.

But when Mamma suggested placing the statue up high on a shelf, where all could see, Niccolò refused. The gift was for him. "*Take care of her*," Papà had said. And so Niccolò would.

"*Che male?*" said Nonno. "What harm can come of it?" But Mamma wasn't sure, given the temperature of the times.

"Keep it safe," said Mamma.

I promise, said Niccolò.

Liberty! Proof of America! Never had the boy felt so empowered. He would make Papà proud. He would show it to everyone.

At school, Maestra Leonora had Niccolò stand with his statue and tell the class about New York, where everything moved very fast and not everyone was to be trusted. In Church, the Monsignore seemed disappointed the statue wasn't a rosary; nevertheless, he was impressed by her flaming torch and her vague resemblance to St. Sebastian, whose final agonies appeared on the sacristy wall. Niccolò showed the statue to everyone in the bakery; to the widows at the well; and to his friends, some of whom attempted to peek under her robes, which led to words, which led to a fistfight, but no harm done, and Liberty's honor remained unsullied.

But after one or two customers at the bakery had leaned across the counter to whisper hints to Mamma; after Nonno had overheard grumblings from Fabbro the stablemaster at Biggio's barbershop; after several of Niccolo's older schoolmates who were now members of the *Balilla* made remarks to their teachers, Mamma once again suggested putting the statue back on a shelf.

"Why?" said Niccolo.

"It's safer here," replied Mamma.

"He gave it to me to take care of," said Niccolo. "*A me.*"

Nonno snorted; Mamma gave him a look.

A compromise was reached. Onto Niccolo's pants Mamma sewed a pocket large enough to conceal the statue.

"Show it to no one," she said. "*Promessa di me.*"

"I promise" said Niccolo.

Why not? Everyone had seen it already.

SUMMER BEGAN, draping the town in a blanket of heat. Piazza Piccola baked in the sun, giving off its heady perfume of dust, goats, horse manure and sweat. Morelli the vegetable seller and his horse, who had no name, stood motionless amid a hovering cloud of flies. Fausto the fool lay panting in the shade and did not sweep. In the bakery Mamma sighed as she kneaded the dough while Nonno, in the storeroom, worked stripped to the waist, his tiny frame stringed with sinew as he hauled sacks of flour. As usual, everyone complained. As usual, no one had a solution. For Niccolò's friends, however –at least, those not at camp – there were diversions.

"*Eccola!*" whispered Rinaldo, jerking his head. "There she is!" Around the fountain half a dozen boys gathered to catch a cooling spray of mist, followed Rinaldo's glance to the *macelleria* – the butcher shop – where a woman, old to the boys but young to the world, had appeared in the doorway.

"Did I tell you?" bragged Rinaldo. "*Magnifico!*"

The woman, hips swiveling, leaned against the doorframe, raising one arm to push back her luxuriant hair. Underneath, her neck glistened with sweat; under her arms, dark stains. Her dress clung to her body. She sighed and closed her eyes – whether out of boredom, fatigue, or despair – and turned her face to the hint of breeze through the doorway.

"Who is she?" asked Quindici.

"The butcher's wife," said Rinaldo. "Most of the time he keeps her trapped inside so no one can see."

"Why?"

"He thinks somebody might steal her."

To Niccolò this made no sense. "They can't steal her," he said. "She's the wife."

Rinaldo shook his head in disgust; then a faraway look came into his eye. He spoke in barely a whisper. "I've seen her naked," he said.

The reaction was as he'd hoped: stunned, awestruck silence.

"Have not!" said Nardo, who, though younger than Rinaldo, had come to rival him in size. Unfazed, Rinaldo smiled.

"She takes a bath. Every afternoon. One o'clock. I've seen through her window, in the alley. Lots of times."

In that instant, in the eyes of the boys at the fountain, the woman in the doorway became something new: no longer a mere butcher's wife, but a promise; a mystery; a secret thrill; a forbidden itch.

75

"Prove it," said Nardo. "Tomorrow. Take us there."

It was clear a challenge had been issued. Rinaldo shrugged, spat. "Why should I?"

At that very moment Jacopo Scarpacci – the butcher himself – appeared in the doorway: swarthy, huge, hairy, his hands seemingly as big as the carcasses of the beasts and small boys who, it was said, hung from his butcher's hooks. With a growl to his wife - who turned, unfazed, sullen, and went in - Scarpacci launched a warning glare across the piazza; by the time it reached the fountain, however, no one was there to receive it. The boys had scattered. Still, in an instant the enterprise had been set, the participants sworn to secrecy. If all went as planned, the next day the boys would see Scarpacci's wife, *au naturel,* unsuspecting, in her bath.

Niccolò was not so sure he would go.

"What's wrong with you?" said Quindici. "Chicken?"

It wasn't quite that. To Niccolò, the youngest of the group, the adventure seemed a waste of an afternoon. What was so special about baths? He had often seen Mamma in hers. In fact, the thought of his friends, especially Rinaldo, spying on Mamma, made him clench his fists in fury.

And yet.

The butcher's wife was not Mamma. Niccolò thought of the secret thrill that had run through the group. There it was again: the mystery. Mamma, Maestra Leonora, the Virgin Mary, now Scarpacci's wife. Confusion.

Here was a chance to clear matters up.

"Have you ever seen a woman naked?" he said to Grandfather that evening. "Who wasn't your mother?"

Nonno laughed until tears came to his eyes. But Mamma, who had overheard, sent Niccolò to bed without supper.

So the next afternoon Niccolò went.

THE EXPEDITION turned out to be more fun than Niccolò had imagined, like playing *nascondino* – follow-the-leader – in places he'd never been. Led by Rinaldo, seven young boys (their number had grown overnight) set off for the alley behind the *macelleria*, taking a circuitous route to avoid undue attention. As they went, climbing fences, cutting through yards, avoiding barking dogs, Piazza Piccola lifted her skirts to reveal her hidden secrets – rusting washbasins, ancient chicken coops, lines hung with undergarments. By the time they'd topped the wall behind the *macelleria*, Niccolò had nearly forgotten why they had come. Then he remembered.

"There," whispered Rinaldo, pointing.

Before them lay the yard. The gates, through which weekly truckloads of carcasses arrived, were locked; by the doorway lay piles of scraps and tubs of offal, awaiting disposal. In one corner, near the barn, a brindle dog lay chained, growling unhappily in its sleep. Rinaldo motioned toward a fire escape that led to a second floor window.

"That's where she does it," he murmured.

From the window came a faint wisp of steam, carrying with it the imagined scent of forbidden perfumes, female emanations – the incense of lust wafting across a yard full of animal intestines. It made Niccolò dizzy.

"What about the dog?" whispered Quindici.

"Don't worry, he's old and deaf," said Rinaldo.

Nardo nodded. "Okay, then, let's go."

"You go. I'll keep watch," said Rinaldo.

Instinctively, a tremor of suspicion ran through the group.

"You're not coming?" frowned Nardo. "Why not?"

Rinaldo spat over his shoulder. "I've seen. A million times." He shifted his weight and shrugged. Among the boys on the wall grew an uneasy silence. Nardo's eyes narrowed.

"What's wrong with a million and one?" he said.

Rinaldo just looked at the sky. The only sound was the *chock-chock-chock* of the dog sharpening his skills in his sleep.

Nardo toed some pebbles and eyed the window, as if weighing the arguments. "You sure you've been up there? That window? And you've seen her? Naked?"

"Look" snapped Rinaldo, turning the full force of his seniority on the younger boy, "I did you a favor, bringing you here. You don't wanna go, no skin off me, *capito?*"

Perhaps some months earlier the ploy might have worked, the status quo preserved, Rinaldo's leadership unchallenged. Over the past months, however, Nardo had grown both in stature and confidence. Now, it was clear, a moment of crisis had arrived. Nardo cocked his head, fixed his older rival with a hard stare.

"You've never seen her at all, have you? You don't even know if she's there."

A second passed. Another. Rinaldo looked away. "That's what I heard, anyway."

With that, the mantle of leadership passed. Nardo glanced once more at the window, then spat over his shoulder.

"Who's coming with me?" he said, and jumped off the wall.

Everyone, including Rinaldo, followed.

There are moments in every boy's life that etch themselves in memory; moments of happiness, grief, or abject fear. For Niccolò, the journey across the butcher's back yard took place in a haze of heart-stopping terror. All that kept him from bolting was the promise of a reward more compelling than the warnings of his pounding heart: a clue to the mystery neither priest nor grandfather could explain. Indeed, by the time the sleeping dog had been skirted, the steps of the fire escape mounted - not without a good deal of pushing and whispered bickering - the answer at last seemed at hand. Now, a code would be broken; a rite of manhood completed.

They reached the window.

Silently, the boys took up positions, Niccolò and Quindici standing on tiptoe to peer through the layer of dust and grime that clung to most windows, indeed to everything on Piazza Piccola. And what they saw promised to exceed their expectations. Wrapped in a cloud of steam, she lay submerged in her bathwater; glistening, insouciant, idle, carelessly vulnerable to their ravenous glances.

"What did I tell you?" whispered Rinaldo, who had been the last up the stairs.

"*Sta' zitto!*" hissed Nardo. "You're lucky I let you be here at all." Niccolò, his eyes fixed on the scene within, heard none of this. All he knew was a mounting excitement as the figure in the bathtub reached for her towel. Rising from the water like Venus from the sea, she turned, at last revealing her perfect nakedness.

Swarthy.

Mustachioed.

Hands like ham hocks.

Among other things.

"*Il macellario!*"

The butcher! At the sound of strangled cries outside his bathroom window, Jacopo Scarpacci, wrapped in his towel, turned to glimpse a half-dozen small faces, contorted in horror. What followed – the rattling of footsteps on the fire escape, the snarling of the awakened brindle dog, the frantic flight of terrified boys down alleyways, through gardens, across fences, could only be compared to the scampering of rabbits before the jaws of a hungry wolf. As fast as the boys ran, faster in pursuit came Scarpacci himself, still grasping his towel, cleaver in hand, intent on chopping at least one of his tormentors into pieces, his furious bellow echoing like a bull in heat. Into the square spilled the pursuit, boys fanning out in all directions, frantically seeking escape, concealment or sanctuary – all but Nardo, who in order to save the others, turned and offered himself up to Scarpacci's furious grasp. But this part Niccolò had not seen.

For Niccolò, the flight from the butcher's back yard – indeed, the sight of the butcher himself, transformed in an instant from shimmering goddess to hairy beast – had been bad enough. Fear had given him wings as he flew down the alley, heart exploding in his throat, afraid to look back, aware only of his own high-pitched screams and the possibility of sudden extinction. Then, miraculously, Piazza Piccola opened her arms in front of him – directly across, just beyond the statue of Garibaldi, lay the bakery. Home! Safety! Mamma!

Then he tripped.

One foot, then the other, stumbling, gasping, down he went, coat flying open, sprawling helplessly onto the pavement. The bite of the rocks against his palms, tearing at his pants. At that moment, all the forces of despair seemed to hover above him, mocking his puny attempts to manage the dismal vocabulary of life: lust, nakedness, Maestra Leonora, the butcher's wife...

...Liberty. Skittering away across the stones.

The pocket Mamma had knitted came apart as Niccolò fell; out flew the statue, forgotten for weeks, spinning, whirling beyond the boy's frantic grasp. Loosed from her shadows, Liberty gleamed in the sunlight; then, still spinning, she made contact with the curb. Niccolò heard the crack of the metal, saw the statue break in two. The larger part bounced and came to rest; the smaller, comprised of the head, continued along the curb, rattling tinnily onto the open grillwork of a storm drain.

For an instant, the proud head turned toward the sky, as if nodding a gallant farewell.

Then it teetered and tumbled into the drain.

THE WEATHER CONTINUED hot and dry; an air of exhaustion settled onto the square. The usual tempo of argument, insult and bickering – the pulse of Piazza Piccola – slowed to an exhausted truce, under which the occurrences at Scarpacci's back window caused barely a stir. At the well the widow Petacci, who oversaw the allocation, relevance, and disbursement of all local gossip, dismissed the event as *di nessun valore*. Boys, after all, would be boys.

Nardo, for his part, received two beatings: one from the butcher (although not with his cleaver), another that night from his father; all of which served to cement his role as the new *capo* of the group, with a full complement of welts and bruises to confirm his office. As for Rinaldo, whose idea the whole thing had been, his face was not seen in the square for weeks; it would be months before his reputation could be repaired. For the rest of the boys – once the immediate terror had waned – the adventure was recounted, boasted about, then quickly forgotten.

As for Scarpacci's wife, her honor remained inviolate. So the matter was laid to rest.

For everyone but Niccolò.

Day after day, under the punishing sun, a small boy could be seen squatting in the shadows of the statue of Garibaldi, sometimes accompanied by friends, more often by himself, peering intently through the bars of the massive iron grate that lay along the curb. Day after day, the boy would lower strings, wires, hooks, gum, in a futile attempt to reach a treasure lying wedged between the stones at the bottom of the storm drain. Perhaps, had the weather been cooler, Mamma, glancing out the bakery window, might have questioned her son's behavior, but the shop was busy, and the heat from the oven oppressive, and the news from Rome and America distracted her thoughts. Besides, as was said, boys will be boys. *Non importa.*

"What's the big thing?" said Quindici, squatting with Niccolò. "Tell them you lost it," he said. "They'll get you a new one."

The trouble was, Niccolò had not yet learned to lie. Certainly not to Papà. "*Take care of her*" the card had said. His father had trusted him and now he had betrayed that trust. Now the proof of the betrayal lay broken and exposed, out of reach, one eye peering upward in mute accusation, while the rest of the corpse, headless and obscene, lay hidden behind sacks of flour in the back of the bakery storehouse. Sooner or later, Mamma would ask. Then what would he say?

One evening the long and unbearable heat spell broke. A powerful crash of lightning above the Grand Hotel Imperiale introduced the event. Within minutes, a pounding storm had rumbled down from the hills, lashing Piazza Piccola with sheets of soothing rain, kicking up curtains of mist that whirled across the square in spiraling, almost ghostlike forms. Across the square people rushed for cover, soaked by the time they got there. Despite the rain windows were thrown open to the gusts of cool air. The hot stone pavement breathed a sigh of relief. In the lighted bakery a small crowd gathered, refugees from the wet, delighted to find themselves stranded for the moment. Mamma was handing out complimentary *biscotti*; there was happy laughter and chatter. Niccolò stood at the window, watching the raindrops race and merge and race faster down the pane, while outside, a corona of light from the window spilled a warm glow into the darkness.

It was then, as he watched, that at the very edge of the light a figure appeared, diaphanous, barely discernible, but there all the same: a woman, naked and pale.

For a moment she hovered, silent, as the raindrops danced at her feet. Her eyes found Niccolò; he raised his arm to touch the window.

Then she was gone.

Liberty.

She had come stripped of her robes, without her torch, in her full womanhood, her nakedness revealed. She had come whole and resurrected. She had come to accuse.

Niccolò turned from the window. At the counter, Mamma was smiling. Someone had told a joke and everyone was amused. Inside the bakery, on this night, the world was familiar, known, comforting. Things made sense.

But outside, in the dark expanse of the Piazza; along the alleys, through windows; in the cruel expressions of young boys; in the slogans shouted by the black-shirted youths at the *caffè*; in the mysteries of virgins and martyrs and sex; outside was another world, baleful, stern, furtive, unforgiving.

Sooner or later his secret would be discovered.

Then what?

LA PASSEGGIATA

Around evening the long day, which began with such promise, staggers to an end and lays down exhausted in the dust, a single step short of victory. In the fading light Donati the goatherd urges his stragglers across the uncrowded square. The final customer climbs from Biggio's barber chair. In the bakery Mamma sets the last of the breads to cool, wipes her hands on her apron, and goes about preparing Niccolo's supper. The sun relinquishes her territories. The streetlights come on. For the briefest part of an hour stillness settles across the Piazza.

Then, so it seems to the boy, a sort of miracle. The nightly *passeggiata* begins. From doorways and alleyways, down the hilly streets that led to the square, the citizens of Piazza Santa Caterina Piccola appear, arm-in- arm, transformed by the advent of evening. Combed, bathed and scented, they stroll past the shops, greeting friends, sharing gossip, defying the day's disappointments, their laughter rising among pools of electric light.

Everyone comes, to see and be seen: bachelors seeking brides; girls with their secret smiles; widows and widowers, lechers and prudes, husbands and wives who walked without saying a word. From apartment windows flows music: Puccini, Caruso, Benny Goodman, Louis Armstrong; opera and jazz, on gramophones and radio sets. In the lambent air the melodies blend together, at once discordant and triumphant, hovering over the murmur of voices below. To Niccolo it seems as if a greater hand is at work, a painter's brush, softening the light, deepening the hues, rendering each woman more profound, each man less coarse - precisely as, at their best, they wish to be.

Later, behind closed doors, among squalling children and the burdens of labor and debt, the endless bickering resumes; the furtive coupling; the drunken cruelties; the slap of hand across face; the muffled cries of loneliness and loss. But for now, in this single, beatified hour, part of a tradition more beautiful than themselves, the people walk and the music plays; while, far off, wolves howl in the darkened mountains.

THE NAMES OF LOVE

I t was once well known on Piazza Santa Caterina Piccola that Claudio Scarpone, the blacksmith's son, and Beatrice Aquilina, the seamstress's daughter, had met by chance on the road into town one June afternoon and fallen in love. *Un colpo di fulmine*. Like lightning.

This was a long time ago.

He had been twenty, she barely seventeen. Being young and beautiful, they held hands and kissed, and made a bed in the leaves and pledged their love to each other for all time.

Then they set about renaming the world.

They did this with names too beautiful to express and impossible for others to understand; names of no known alphabet or derivation; names both meaningful and meaningless at the same time. They renamed the ground on which they lay; the fingers on each other's hands, the breeze that ruffled her hair, the nipples of her breasts, the bee that stung his hand; the kiss she planted there to soothe his exquisite pain.

Of course, they renamed each other, often several times with several names in the very same minute.

But that was just the beginning.

They renamed the tulips on Signora Martelli's front porch, the forty-one sheep in the shepherd's flock, the hat on an old man's head; they even renamed the Widow Caputo's behind as she stooped to wash her laundry at the well. These names made them laugh with delight, and blush at their own indiscretion.

But they didn't stop there.

They renamed the day and the night – especially the night, which they named a thousand blissful times. She renamed his lips, his arms; he her graceful neck and the supple arch of her back. When dawn broke they renamed the sun, the fields, the brooks, the sky, then turned their attention to town. Generations of names were erased within minutes; ancient titles fell within hours. They did this brashly, arrogantly, without regard for anyone's feelings. When they had finished the Piazza shone, gleaming, as if suddenly made new.

There were, naturally, objections.

"What gives them the right to do this?" muttered Ludovici the shopkeeper, after they had renamed every item in his shop. "Someone should stop it," complained la Signorina Tutino the seamstress, who had never been in love and resented anyone who had.

Even Claudio's father, Pietro the blacksmith, who was wise in the ways of the world, felt a twinge of concern. "I suspect they have been bewitched," he growled.

Which, in a way, was true.

The only ones who had nothing to say on the matter were the old people who sat together late afternoons in the lengthening shadows of the square, listening, hearing the names as if they were echoes from distant mountains. Perhaps they knew better about things like this.

In any event, there was no stopping it.

Claudio and Beatrice renamed sorrow until it was bliss, pain until it was joy. They renamed the long hours apart from each other as trials of the heart. They renamed the plighting of their troths; and when the day of their marriage came they banished that name with another as they took their vows before family and God.

And that night, husband and wife at last, having together renamed the world, they fell asleep in each other's arms.

Out of sheer exhaustion.

CLAUDIO AND BEATRICE moved into a small apartment on the Via Giuseppe Mazzini, just off Piazza Piccola. With the bride's dowry they purchased a bed; from the groom's father came a handcrafted cradle for the child who was already expected. Beatrice set up housekeeping; Claudio returned to work at the shop. At night they spent time with friends, laughed, celebrated, got drunk, made love. They were happy. They no longer made up names, however. There was no need; the ones they had were more than enough to suffice.

In less than a year the cradle was filled with a child; three more years and the family numbered five. There were fevers and colds and groceries to buy. Beatrice's father took sick. The blacksmith business faltered, a victim of modern times. Claudio began to train as a mechanic. Given all this, the names the two lovers had cherished began to seem unimportant, even trivial. Their own children squealed in embarrassment to hear them used.

So, gradually they stopped using them.

In fact, as the years went by they began to forget the names altogether. Those they recalled, on the few occasions when they did, no longer made sense and sounded only vaguely familiar, like the remembered voices of acquaintances one knew briefly, and only once, a lifetime ago.

Then an odd thing happened. Their children, now grown, met lovers on the road outside of town and went about renaming the very things Claudio and Beatrice had named many years before. They did this brashly, arrogantly, without regard for anyone's feelings. And when they had finished, the town once again gleamed with a new brightness. The names their parents had once invented were simply tossed away, but no one noticed except for the old people who sat together on late afternoons in the lengthening shadows of the piazza, who were not the same old people who had sat there years ago, but who listened all the same.

THE CHILDREN grew older; there were arguments and funerals; life spilled out its cornucopia of missed opportunities, hopes curtailed, wrinkles and uncertain fate. Against this tide of loss, Claudio and Beatrice stood together, side by side, as one. The very things they had once renamed – people, places, landmarks, events – things that once had been so vibrant, slipped from importance, then from existence, then, at last, from recollection. Buried beneath the weight of the present, the last of the lovers' names was forgotten.

Then for a very long while Claudio and Beatrice were old and sat together in the lengthening shadows, listening as new names replaced the ones before, which had replaced the ones before that. There were, naturally, objections from some; but they stayed silent.

Gradually, the world receded. Things fell away and became small, reduced to a single room, and Time delivered them, inexorably, unto that terrible hour of Death.

And here was a miracle. As the priest stood in the darkened room administering his oils, the door wreathed in crepe, in the silence around Claudio and Beatrice the old names came alive again, brilliant and shining, glorious in their power. On his deathbed, Claudio whispered them to Beatrice and she back to him. With the saying of names, they grew young again.

She kissed his hand. And they renamed Death with a name so beautiful it could not, not ever, be changed.

And that name, the very last, remains to this day.

THE MAN WHO WAS
NOT JOHN GILBERT

Antonio Marchioni was a handsome man; some would say the handsomest on Piazza Piccola. With his dazzling smile, swept back hair, pencil-thin mustache and slender physique, who could fail to notice him on the evening *passeggiata*, standing out from the usual rabble of burghers and farmers to whom nature, for reasons of her own, had been less generous in her gifts?

Indeed, Fortune had blessed Antonio all his life.

From the day of his birth, his mother doted on him; his sisters showered him with unending rivers of favors and delights. As boyhood turned to manhood, Antonio's blessings multiplied. By his fourteenth birthday he'd been bedded by half a dozen of his sisters' friends. By seventeen, hardly a *signorina* remained who hadn't shared his favors in bedroom, hayloft, or even the balcony of the recently renamed *Cinema Duce*. People were drawn to him; employers lined up to offer him work. All these beatitudes Antonio accepted without question. If Fate had chosen him, who was he to argue? Antonio Marchioni believed in Fate.

But on the night of his 18th birthday all that changed.

That evening Antonio, in the company of a stunning young woman whose name hardly matters now, arrived at the aforementioned *Cinema Duce* to enjoy, along with an overflow crowd, the much–anticipated premiere of "Monte Cristo," the heart-pounding saga of Edmond Dantes, the heroic Count of Monte Cristo. It being Antonio's birthday, and the girl being beautiful, one can only surmise the young man's expectations as the lights came down and the accompanist, Isobel Andoloro, in her sparkling tiara, began to play.

Then the movie began.

There, on the flickering screen, towering twice the size of ordinary mortals, appeared the actor playing Edmond Dantes. The audience gasped: by any measure, this was a handsome man, with his dazzling smile, piercing eyes, swept back hair, pencil-thin mustache and slender physique. Handsome, and yet...somehow familiar. Within seconds whispers were heard in the audience. Heads began to turn in Antonio's direction. Within minutes the murmurs threatened to drown out the accompanist's music. Indeed, by the time Edmund Dantes made his heroic escape from prison in a burial sack, a single astonishing coincidence had become impossible to ignore. The fact was that the actor on screen so resembled Antonio Marchioni in face and form, as to be his exact twin; a duplicate; a *doppelgänger*.

The likeness was, to put it mildly, uncanny.

Who was this celluloid hero? None other than John Gilbert, the swashbuckling star of such stirring films as "Ben Hur" and the smoldering "Flesh and the Devil," the real-life paramour of such Hollywood goddesses as Mary Pickford and Greta Garbo. This was the man the movie magazines had dubbed "The Great Lover." This was the man Antonio resembled, but was not.

In the blink of an eye, his face no longer belonged to him. From that night, as fate would have it, Antonio Marchioni of Piazza Piccola ceased to be.

He had become the Man Who Looked Like John Gilbert.

THE REPERCUSSIONS did not take long to make themselves felt. At first, as possessor of John Gilbert's face, Antonio found he had acquired a certain panache in the minds of his neighbors and friends. The similarity was, after all, remarkable, the novelty intriguing; for some days on Piazza Piccola, it was the sole topic of discussion. Soon, however, a reaction set in, a feeling that, somehow, the Man Who Looked like John Gilbert but was not, was, to put it politely, an imposter. It was, after all, unnerving to find oneself face to face with someone whose face purported to be one man's, but was in fact another man's altogether; no matter if that man had been known, admired and trusted for years. In a very short time, people began to feel as if they'd been tricked. Invitations fell off. Greetings went unacknowledged. When Antonio passed former friends on the street, they looked away, as if repulsed by some disfigurement; as if he were the victim of some terrible accident.

Which, in a sense, he was.

The jobs he had been offered melted away. The women who'd swooned at his very glance no longer acknowledged his presence. His mother, claiming illness, took to her bed. His brothers, needless to say, rejoiced. To Antonio, who had spent his life believing himself Fortune's favorite, this sudden reversal came as a blow. Seeking answers, he fled to the confessional of the Church of San Bartolomeo Giusto.

"Is it a sin," he whispered to Monsignore Don Federico, "To look like someone else?"

Don Federico paused to consider, then delivered his verdict. "Resemblance," he intoned, "Is the father of Vanity, the cousin of Deceit, the stepchild of Lust. Avoid it like the plague."

Failing to find relief in the Church, Antonio boarded a train for Rome, the movie capital of Italy. Here, he reasoned, his looks, which on Piazza Piccola had become a detriment, were bound to stand him in good stead. If he had to live with movie-star looks, he could at least put them to use as an actor.

Within a week he'd returned home. The movies, he had been informed, already had a man who looked like John Gilbert: in this case John Gilbert himself.

Feeling increasingly redundant, Antonio resorted to more drastic measures. But despite his best efforts to alter his looks – shaving his mustache, growing a beard, pretending to walk with a limp – despite all this he succeeded only in looking, in the eyes of the populace of Piazza Piccola, like a bearded, limping John Gilbert.

In desperation, he considered entering a monastery. The Abbot of Abbazia di San Giuda, however, having seen the real John Gilbert star with Greta Garbo in the searing "Flesh and the Devil," rejected Antonio's application, fearing his looks would distract the other monks, though whether they also had seen "Flesh and the Devil," and why, was never explained.

Gradually Antonio began to accept his lot. Perhaps, he surmised, it was Fortune's little joke that an image no more substantial than a beam of light had, from half a world away, condemned him to be forever recognized as someone else. Perhaps, he reasoned, all this might yet be prelude to some greater destiny. It was simply a matter of accepting one's fate.

Which is why, when he heard of an opening at the Grand Hotel Imperiale, the position of nighttime telephone switchboard operator, he didn't hesitate.

He jumped at the chance.

IN THOSE DAYS TELEPHONES were rare on Piazza Piccola: what use was a phone in a place where everyone already knew everyone else's business? Nevertheless, the proprietors of the Grand Hotel Imperiale, hoping to draw a more cosmopolitan class of guest, installed in the lobby a switchboard of the most up-to-date specifications; which, when unveiled, caused such a stir that for weeks the local citizenry stood in line to gawk at this gleaming technological wonder. By the time Antonio reported for work, however, the novelty had worn off, so that as he was issued his switchboard operator's cap – not so different from a ship's radio operator's cap at sea –

he found himself alone at his post in a far corner of the lobby, for all intents abandoned and invisible. Which was exactly as he wished.

The job was neither difficult nor busy, though it had moments of excitement, as when a drunken diplomat, no doubt despondent to find himself stranded on Piazza Piccola, took out his anger on the ballroom chandelier with a set of dueling pistols. In addition there was the puzzling demise, in the rooms above, of a celebrated general at the hands of the Sisters of the Convent Figlie del Sacro Cuore di Gesù. But these were isolated events. As a rule Antonio's nights consisted of fielding no more than a dozen calls and completing the required connections; mercifully, all without the complications of face-to face interaction.

And if his hours were lonely, if his heart ached for remembered friends and companionship, at least Antonio was spared the agony of being the object of other people's disappointment. Gradually, like a prisoner shut away in a dungeon, he gave up hope of ever seeing the light of day.

Naturally, it was then that Fate, ever inscrutable, conspired to reconnect him.

This time, long distance.

"PER FAVORE," said the female voice on the line. "Connect me to Room 351."

"*Un momento*," replied Antonio, making the desired connection. It being nearly midnight, he stayed on the line while the phone rang in Room 351. When, after several rings, there had been no response, Antonio cleared his throat. "I regret to say your party is not answering," he said.

"Let it ring, if you please," said the voice.

"*Certamente*," replied Antonio, and did. After half a dozen more rings, however, it seemed appropriate to state the obvious. "I'm afraid your party does not appear to be in. Or, perhaps, has gone to bed. Shall I take a message?" he said.

From the other end of the line he heard a sob, then a cry of despair. Then, a click as the line went dead.

This being a hotel, such things were not unusual: clean towels and despair are a regular feature of hotels. Still, something about the woman's voice struck a chord in Antonio's heart, so that when on the following night he heard the voice again, he immediately recognized it. Again, she requested room 351; again the phone rang unanswered. "Perhaps I may take a message?" said Antonio, half-dreading a repetition of the previous night's sob.

"Yes," said the voice. "You may tell the man in 351 that tonight I will take my life."

"That, in my opinion," said Antonio, "Would be a shame."

"Perhaps," said the voice. "But the fact is my heart is broken."

"Hearts can mend," said Antonio.

"I have lost all hope," said the voice.

"A different matter altogether," said Antonio, "One with which I have had some experience. Can you hold for one moment?"

"Be quick," said the voice "I have things to do."

Hastily Antonio fielded another call, gathered his thoughts and returned to the party who had lost all hope, and who, he had already decided, must be young, possibly attractive, certainly a good conversationalist.

"Still there?" he ventured.

"What does a man like yourself know about hopelessness?" said the young woman (if that indeed was who she was).

97

Sure of his subject, Antonio explained: the ache of loneliness, the sorrow of lost friends, the betrayal of family, the bitter turnings of Fate. He did this without once mentioning his resemblance to the actor John Gilbert which, he told himself, would only muddy the waters. He spoke for some time, pausing only to field the occasional call and remind the night janitor that the lobby ashtrays required attention. When he had finished, there was silence on the line.

"Still there?" he said.

"Thank you," said the voice, and the line went dead; but not before Antonio was struck with a sense that the light had returned to his life. He felt his heart rising from the ashes. He only hoped she would call again.

Which she did, the next night, and the night that followed.

Her name, she told him, was Ginevra. Her family home was Ravenna, but more recently she'd lived and worked in Milan. Now that the ice had been broken they talked of everything: art, faith, literature, politics along with, naturally, hope. She mentioned the man in room 351, whom she did not love but who, after many years of seeking and not finding, she had decided was preferable to a life of loneliness; and who – Antonio had checked – had left the hotel soon after her phone calls and not left a forwarding address.

"I am finished with him forever," Ginevra announced. "I prefer to believe there is better in the world."

Grateful to have a connection at last, to be taken for who he was, Antonio blossomed. He found himself resenting other calls that came in to the switchboard, particularly from the guest in the recently renamed *Duce* Suite who insisted on ordering room service long after room service had closed for the night. Occasionally, when the discussions with Ginevra were most intense, Antonio would shut down the rest of the switchboard to concentrate on her alone. Restless all day, he craved the hour when, in the deep of night, the panel would glow with her call.

"Ginevra" he found himself singing, over and over.

This continued for some days. As their talks became more intimate, Antonio and Ginevra discovered they shared the same opinions and tastes on a range of subjects. They each revered Dante, for example, but abhorred Thomas Mann. They agreed on the ideal number of children (four), and the perfect place to vacation (Corfù, though neither had been there). More than once they agreed that love conquered all. And though on occasion it occurred to Antonio to introduce the subject of Hollywood actors, John Gilbert among them; then tactfully segue to the coincidence of his own physiognomy, about which they might have a good laugh and move on, he did not.

Until it was too late.

"Do you think we shall ever meet?" uttered Ginevra one night, sometime just after two.

At the switchboard Antonio panicked. "*Un momento,*" he stammered. Placing Ginevra on hold, he considered his options. Even now, he might tell the truth, throw caution to the wind and hope for the best. He reconnected the line

"At the moment, I'm afraid I can't travel," he explained. "My job requires I stay where I am."

"Not to worry," said Ginevra. "I'm happy to come to you."

"*Un attimo,*" said Antonio, and again placed her on hold. Ripples of terror lapped at his feet.

"You know, I've been meaning to ask," he said, off-handedly, as if the thought had just popped into his head, "Who, if any, is your favorite movie actor?"

"Why?" she inquired.

"No reason," he said.

"John Gilbert, I suppose," Ginevra replied, and Antonio felt a trapdoor fall open beneath his feet. He could think of nothing more to say. The long silence that followed seemed an eternity.

"Is there someone else in your life?" ventured Ginevra at last.

"No," bleated Antonio.

"Perhaps, then, you will have the good grace to tell me why --"

Antonio cut the connection.

After a moment, the line rang again, and again after that. Each time he let it ring. It rang until dawn, when it finally stopped. Of the hundreds of calls to pass through the switchboard of the Grand Hotel Imperiale in the following days, none were from Ginevra. Too late Antonio realized that in all the months before it had been she who had called him; he had never asked for her number. Nor in any case, would he have dared to call her back. What would he say, having so deftly and utterly caused her humiliation?

Night after night in the lobby of the Grand Hotel Imperiale Antonio watched the janitor empty ashtrays as he reflected on what he had thrown away. Gradually it became clear he would never again lay eyes on the woman he had never laid eyes on, but had fallen in love with all the same.

MONTHS PASSED. While in Hollywood the career of the man who was John Gilbert continued to blossom, so on Piazza Piccola did the man who was not John Gilbert fall deeper into anonymity. Antonio's reluctance to be seen in public became an abhorrence of all human company. He no longer ventured outside his apartment in daylight; when the bell to his apartment rang, he hid in the closet. At the switchboard in the lobby of the Grand Hotel Imperiale he took to wearing a fedora one size too large, pulled low on his brow. In time, his only connection to the world of human intercourse was his voice on the telephone, even that late at night, when most of the world had gone to sleep. Which is why, when a stranger approached him one evening and spoke to him directly, Antonio was at a loss.

"Do I have the honor of addressing the night hotel operator?" said the stranger, a gentleman of some evident means.

For a moment Antonio was silent, having grown unused to actual conversation. "*Sì*," he croaked, wishing only to be invisible.

The man gestured to the switchboard. "Then it is you whose voice I hear on this telephone?"

"It is," answered Antonio, now recognizing the stranger's voice as that of the man who insisted on ordering room service even when there was none.

"In that case," said the fellow, "Perhaps I may interest you in a proposition."

"Dinner is not available after midnight," replied Antonio.

"That aside," said the stranger, "Have you considered a career in communications?"

"No one," said Antonio. "Wants another John Gilbert."

"I am unfamiliar with the name," remarked the gentleman. "My interests lie solely in the field of radio broadcasting, the modern wonder invented by our own Guglielmo Marconi, which may be said to have bound the great world together in these tenuous times. Radio, as you may surmise, requires voices: as a guest in this hotel, I have had the pleasure of hearing yours, across these very wires. For some time I have searched for just such a voice: one forged in suffering, tempered by disappointment and rich with the very marrow of life." At which, the man paused for a breath.

"You should know," said Antonio, "That I am a coward who has, out of vanity, sacrificed all, including love."

"It is not your courage that interests me. Only your voice," said the man, handing Antonio his card.

"I am Fortune's whipping boy," said the Man Who Looked Like John Gilbert.

"Then," said the other, "You have nothing to lose."

THUS ONCE AGAIN the winds of Fate conspired to fill Antonio's sails, this time with a hurricane of unforeseen success. His journey from the backwaters of Piazza Piccola to the studios of Radio Rai Internazionale in Rome, where he quickly became a rising star in the burgeoning new medium, has by now been well documented and celebrated. Within the year, thousands of Antonio's countrymen heard his voice as he read the news, spoke with political leaders, and issued advice to listeners; within five years powerful transmitters were beaming his signature sound – now referred to as the *Forte Marchioni* around the world. As the "Voice of Italy," Antonio seemed to embody a national essence, a hopeful despair, the very "marrow of life." The people loved him.

When Italy faltered and war came, and national hope seemed extinguished, it was "Papà Antonio," broadcasting nightly from exile in beleaguered London, who inspired the partisans to throw off their shackles and restore the national pride with his rallying cry of *Qui si fa l'Italia o si muore* - "Here we make Italy or die."

All without showing his face.

Perhaps as remarkably, in yet another of fortune's sleights-of-hand, as Antonio's career in radio blossomed, likewise did the Hollywood fortunes of his *doppelganger* John Gilbert quite suddenly run aground –because of his voice. Audiences around the world, flocking to see the new "talking pictures," were shocked to hear John Gilbert speak in tones which were anything but stirring, or deep, or even rich with the marrow of life. Within months his star had dimmed; within the year his fame and box-office faded. Not long after, in despair, John Gilbert took his own life.

So it was that, in just a few years, the man who was John Gilbert faded from memory, while the man who was not John Gilbert bestrode the world.

BUT LET US PAUSE in this headlong pursuit, which has launched us far beyond the boundaries of the tiny piazza where Antonio, in humbler days, first encountered true love and recklessly tossed it away. Despite his ever-growing fame, his name in lights, the shadow of regret continued to haunt his being. The very name *"Ginevra,"* spoken in a crowd, could send Antonio into paroxysms of despair. Perhaps, he would muse in his private moments, the real Ginevra, whom he had never met, would one day seek him out. But as years went by, though his life was filled with upturned faces both famous and obscure, none of the faces turned out to be hers.

Until, at long last, their wandering paths converged.

"Eccellentissimo!" boomed the Ambassador, steering his way toward Antonio amid the candlelit pomp of a London reception, while outside, the blitz of 1940 beat a deep and relentless tattoo. "Allow me to introduce a countryman of yours – one who, I'm given to understand, has some acquaintance with your town of origin."

The stranger's name, it turned out, was unfamiliar to Antonio.

"Nevertheless," said the man, "I had the privilege – if that is the word – of spending some days at your Grand Hotel Imperiale - if that was the name – some years ago."

"Ah," replied Antonio.

"Hardly memorable, perhaps," said the man. "Except in many ways, it changed my life."

Antonio glanced idly around for an escape.

"It was at that very hotel that I nearly lost the love of my life," said the man. Seeing that Antonio was now listening attentively, he continued. "My callous inattentiveness nearly drove her away. Indeed, for some weeks, I believed it had done so. Then, miraculously, she contacted me."

Antonio turned to leave, but the man had hold of his arm.

"It seemed she had had an epiphany," he continued. "Concerning the nature of love. Exactly what, she has always kept to herself."

"This woman –" began Antonio.

"I won't say I have made all things right, but I believe I have given her a modicum of happiness," said the man.

From the crowd a woman approached.

"Ah" said the man. "Here she is now. Signor Marchioni, meet my wife."

LATER THAT NIGHT Antonio made his way home through the rubble of London and the smoke from the bombs, none of which, though hundreds were dropped, had managed to fall upon the gala reception where, at the sound of her voice, he had known it was her.

"*Buona sera*," she had said to the stranger who stood next to her husband: tall, with piercing eyes, swept back hair, pencil-thin mustache and slender physique. He hadn't spoken; even if he had been able, he would not have dared.

"My dear Ginevra," said the husband, nodding toward Antonio, "This is il Signor Marchioni, whose voice we listen to nightly and know all too well."

Silent, without heartbeat or breath, Antonio bowed. A moment passed, then another. She took a step closer. Another. On her face, puzzlement turned to confusion; confusion to disbelief; then suspicion; betrayal; distrust.

"*È proprio lei?*" she whispered urgently. "Is it you?"

"*Sì.*" replied Antonio. "*Sono io.*" For the briefest moment, he forlornly hoped Fate would perhaps effect a *coup.*

She reached up, angrily. Grabbing his face in her hands, she snarled. "*Dunque, è per questo?*" she said. "Because of this? For this small vanity, this *stupidata*, you threw away love?" She raised her fists and shook them. "*Vigliacco!*" she spat. "May you choke on your pride!"

Whereupon she turned and, taking the arm of her husband – the man from Room 351, the man for whom she had settled, foregoing a life of love – Ginevra moved across the floor, through a forest of chosen and elegant guests, many of whom turned to glance in surprise at a woman who, as people so often commented, bore a striking resemblance to the Hollywood actress Clara Bow.

The likeness was uncanny.

⌒

PERHAPS IT WAS that very night, while London burned (as in time, far away, would Piazza Santa Caterina Piccola), that Antonio Marchioni came to an understanding: that Fate, contrary to every expectation, is nothing more than a blind idiot, a lunatic soothsayer, a fool with no plan.

Realizing this, he made his peace.

CAT'S EYE

L ate at night on Piazza Piccola, long after the shops have closed, when the rattling of plates and raucous laughter from the *caffè* have lingered, then diminished, then died; when in the deepening stillness the sighs of the weary earth float upward and disperse; when the moon creeps along the cobblestones beneath Niccolò's window and the whispers of angels flutter across his pillow...

...then comes another sound. The people, cocooned in their dreams, can't hear it.

The cat hears it.

The sound, like a river of night, flows across her fur, restless and electric, crackling with expectation. Her eyes iris open; she stirs and stretches.

Around her the garden is alive with terror and death. She jumps from the window ledge and rubs along the garden wall, ignoring the scurry of mice and small birds in the ivy and the carnage of insects under the leaves. Reaching a hole in the stones she slips through, her tail flipping an arrogant farewell, and is in an instant gone.

Moments later by some alchemy of darkness she rematerializes at the edge of the Piazza, a shadow among shadows, and leaves her scent on the imperceptible breeze: *I am here. Find me if you dare.* From an alley several streets over a tomcat screeches. She knows him: one-eyed, foul-smelling fool. She licks her pads in a show of disinterest, stretches, spine arcing upward, then sets off across the square, alert, wary, unafraid. The cobblestones reek of all that has transpired during the day: the leavings of the vegetable cart, the urine of goats, the noisome foolishness of humans, their comings and goings, their frantic nonsense, their utter waste of time. Of all this she is contemptuous. She lives unfettered by compassion, unburdened by sorrow, impervious to guilt, untroubled by irony. She exists, wholly and completely, in the now.

Do not mistake me.

No matter how you pretend I am yours I am not. I purr from pleasure, not love.

Giving the stone hut of the fool a wide berth – there may be stray dogs inside – she slips down an alley, her mind set on the promise of prey: the butcher's yard. As she does, on the breeze comes the distant yowl of another tom, deeper, menacing, dangerous. This one is new to her, an interloper. A ripple runs down her spine, fear mixed with lust. Tonight she will have her choice of suitors.

Past the stables she tops a wall and looks down into the butcher's yard. It resonates with echoes of slaughter, the thud of the maul, the chop of the cleaver, the gargle of dumb animal fear. In one corner lies the butcher's dog, once fearsome, now old, useless. In nature he would have died long ago but the butcher is not so merciful: the dog lies chained, watching with empty eyes as a rat moves across the yard, fat and arrogant.

The rat has been careless.

In a flash she is airborne, claws extended, hearing her victim's squeal of terror as her shadow descends, feeling it stiffen with panic, spine crunching between her teeth. She drops it; the rat, broken, attempts to crawl away. She drags it back, pinions it, rakes it open with a swipe of claws.

The dog stirs and beats his tail. Across the yard a silhouette has appeared in the moonlight: the one-eyed tom. He screams his arrival, jumps to the yard and sprays. The dog leaps, then yelps as the chain pulls him back. The tom feigns disinterest and sprays again, edging closer to the cat, his single good eye glittering from within his star-shaped black mask.

His smell is obnoxious, familiar. She will not have him. Not again. Not tonight.

She considers her escape and sees none. So be it. She stands her ground and hisses. The tom approaches, one eye a withered kernel.

Fool, he has forgotten how it got that way.

She curls back, spine arched, hackles raised, and spits. The dog is howling now, frantic. Above them a light goes on. The window rattles open. A figure leans out, white in the moonlight. *"Cane rognoso! Stupido! Sta' zitto!"* A heavy boot arcs from the window and strikes the dog with a thump; he yelps a misunderstood protest.

"Basta," cries the butcher's wife. Another boot thumps into the yard, this one aimed at the tom. Distracted, he hesitates.

The cat strikes, ripping his ear.

He screams in agony. She strikes again, raking the mask on his face. Enraged but wounded, tail twitching, he retreats as another boot bounces off his back – the butcher's wife has found the range – and sends him leaping over the wall. In the barn doorway a second figure appears: the butcher, in his nightshirt, rubbing his eyes. The woman picks up another boot.

"*I miei stivali!*" he roars. "My boots!"

She hurls the boot, which lands in a vat of offal near the gate. Now it's the butcher, not the dog, who yelps.

"I warn you!" he bellows.

"*Vaffanculo.*" she sneers.

"*Cagna!*"

"*Bastardo!!!*"

Across the alley another window flies open. "*Scarpacci! Chiudi quella bocca!*" calls an angry voice.

"Mind your own business!" howls the butcher; "*Vaffanculo!*" shouts his wife.

The dog, no longer under bombardment, has resumed his manic fury, rattling against the chain, baying. From down the alley yet another voice chimes in. "*Scarpacci!* Shut up that dog!"

"*Va' a farti fottere!*"

"Who said that?"

"You heard me!"

Fools, all of them.

The cat, silent, scornful, sits unseen in the shadows. She licks her paw and tastes the tom's blood. Next time she will not be so gentle.

She picks up the rat, cradling it tenderly in her mouth, jumps to the wall. In the alley the one-eyed tomcat watches. He has not learned, he will never learn, he cannot. She is in his being. He is her champion.

"Zoccola!" the voice booms outward into the night.

"Stronzo!"

"Sticchio!"

"Piscione!"

⌒

DOWN AN ALLEY past the rusted hulk of an old fire-wagon moldering in the weeds; through an open window comes the howl of an infant, like a newborn kitten. Irritably the cat flicks her tail and changes course into the sacristy garden behind the church.

Inside the sacristy Monsignore Don Federico looks up from his desk, upon which lies next Sunday's sermon, scattered, incomplete, an epic failure. Laboring to conjure the Hand of God in All Things, he has produced nothing more than a shriveled turd. Tonight, it seems, his thoughts are barren, his well of righteousness run dry: perhaps because of his boils, or the rich *ragù di carne* he ate for dinner.

He loosens his vest and belches. Perhaps a further glass of wine would tempt the reluctant muse.

A motion outside the window draws his eye: a cat moves stealthily across the garden. Don Federico taps on the window with his pen; the cat pays no notice. For a moment he envies her, her purity, untroubled by sorrows, unburdened by thought. He wonders briefly if there is room in heaven for cats. (Or, for that matter, for men. Lately – since the episode with the fool on the piazza – he has been having just a modicum of doubt.)

Doubt!

The thought leaps from nowhere. Don Federico quivers with joy: he has found his theme! He will tell of this cat, this omen, this sign from God, this lesson from the natural world; of the miracle of the soul, granted solely to those conceived in His image! The Monsignore takes up his pen and writes. All else forgotten as, outside in the garden, rat's tail dangling from her mouth, the object of his thesis finds her way to the open door of the chapel and slips in.

Inside, the smell of incense, the reek of unrequited hope. At the altar an old woman shuffles, bent over double, sweeping the dust. She has done this for fifty years, now the dust has turned cancerous in her bones. No matter: in this place, she is already halfway to Heaven. She doesn't see the cat approach and peer between the communion rails. Pail in hand the old woman genuflects and moves off down the aisles on ankles like oaken stumps. Before she sleeps she will say a rosary and pray for relief from her pains.

The cat edges through the rails and sits, solitary and small, before the magnificent marble altar. Candlelight gleams from the golden cups and silver vessels, the *paten*, *ostensorium* and *ciborium*. Above, on the canopy, saints and cherubs, inspired, soar upward into Eternity. Between them the naked Christ hangs from nails, eyes wild with pain. For a moment she is transfixed. She thinks of kittens: scrabbling, demanding, insatiable at her nipples.

In the vestibule the old woman sets down her pail.

The cat drops the broken rat upon the altar and disappears through the door.

Darkness pours into the hole of her absence.

ACROSS THE PIAZZA the moonlight has left the cobblestones and climbed the bakery door. In the darkened kitchen the oven ticks softly, even now cooling from its day's long labors. In an alcove behind a figure in a nightshirt lies nearly weightless on a palette, mouth open, toothless, snoring uproariously. Upstairs, beneath a painting of Jesus in Mary's arms, a small boy sleeps in the bed he shares with his mother. She sits at a table across the room, writing. A candle burns, reflected in her mirror. The young woman writes of her loneliness; of running the bakery, pinching pennies, raising a boy to be a man, something she fears she knows nothing about; of the attention of men who daily solicit her; of temptation and yearning; of poisonous gossip, and her own vanity. Is she losing her looks? When the time comes will her husband in America even want her?

She wants to scream, remembering his touch, the bliss of his body inside hers.

Reflected in her mirror the cat appears on a branch outside, as if assembled from shards of moonlight. She has brought a new prize: this time a small thrush, held in her jaws, its tiny heart racing. Already the cat has lost interest; the capture was easy, the bird too small. She sets it beneath her paw and watches as inside the woman balls her fists, brings them down upon her thighs, and lets out a sorrowful moan. The boy in the bed stirs. The woman rises, kneels by his bed and strokes his hair.

The cat lets go of the thrush, which tumbles from the branch. Mid-air its wings flutter. It shoots upward into the night, joyous, chirping a terrified hymn of praise. The cat jumps from the branch, scrambles across the roof tiles and leaps to the ground near the small wooden porch at the bakery's back door. She squeezes through a hole in the boards and disappears under the porch. She has been here before. She is drawn here.

She is not sure why.

Beneath the steps the moonlight lies in stripes on the loamy earth. Crouching low she sniffs the air. The smells are faint but familiar; the smells of a nest, but not in the now, somewhere in the long ago. She sniffs again, whips her tail, skittish, then flattens herself and, gingerly, cautiously, moves further into the shadows.

Here where the moonlight is dim nail heads pierce the boards from above. In the corners lie bones of mice and voles. The center ground, though, has been disturbed. What was here then is now gone. She inches forward, nose twitching, her senses alive. Far in the back, something flutters: the slightest tuft of fur, a wisp, clinging to a protruding nail. She hesitates, then flattens and crawls toward it. Cautious, edgy, front paws planted, she stretches forward as far as she can to sniff.

Kittens.

Hers.

She screams.

In the house, the old man shouts in his sleep.

Under the porch the cat leaps backward, scrambling against the boards of her prison, tearing against the nails. Desperate, she hurtles herself forward, claws at the ground, her yowling now an agonized cry. She finds the escape and leaps through.

The porch door opens. The grizzled old man in his nightshirt, wakened by the bumping beneath, peers into the yard. He sees nothing: the cat is gone, streaking across the cobblestones away from there. The man listens, but now there is only silence. He yawns, smacks his gums, scratches his balls and frowns.

He has been dreaming: a nest of kittens, abandoned. One with a star-shaped mask.

FAUSTO THE FOOL stands in the weeds beneath a canopy of stars. Behind him rise the Roman ruins. His silhouette might be that of a Caesar, architect of empires, seeking victory and truth. But Fausto is not seeking truth; he is looking for stones for his hut. The stones are his truth. They are solid, simple and kind. In summer they keep out the heat, in winter the cold. "*Eccoti, pietra!*" he sings to himself. The stones are his friends. He comes here every night.

Across the field in a patch of long grass the cat sits, panting. She has fled the square, the steps, the nest, the shock of memory. Frantically she grooms herself, but the maddening odor lingers, the sounds of distress, mewling: six of them, warm, tiny, at her nipples. She licks rhythmically, tongue across fur, eyes closed. The motion reassures her, calms her racing heart. The past recedes. The nest recedes. In the now she is safe; in the now she exists, alone, uncompromised.

After a while she crosses a field of large stones, ignoring the fool who sings to the stones. Now she feels hunger. In the ruins perhaps she will find a meal.

A shadow stops her. From the stones ahead struts an enormous tiger cat. All night, he has followed her scent, stalking, waiting. He yowls, powerful, dominating. He is new to these places, down from the hills. He has fought for territory, fought for dominance, fought for lust. He has fought to own her. He reeks of blood. Among the nearby stones, freshly defeated, lies the body of his latest rival, ripped and bleeding. He has tasted victory, now he will claim the prize.

She backs into the grass; he matches her steps. He is twice her size. She spits; he ignores it and brushes past, rubbing against her, confident, strong.

On his fur, she recognizes the smell of his latest battle. Now she knows who lies among the stones.

The tiger doubles back, strutting, rubbing, courting. Despite herself she feels the heat rising; heat, and despair. Dispossessed of another past, she turns and presents herself. He mounts her, howling in pleasure. She feels his claws in her sides, his furious rutting. Unable to stop herself, she sings with pleasure and lust. She remembers nothing but this, this pain, this pleasure. All that exists, or has ever, exists in this now.

Then the tiger is gone among the weeds. She grooms herself beneath the quiet stars. Minutes pass; she feels no hurry. When she has finished her scent is once again hers alone. Only then does she move toward the ruined stones, watchful, searching, already knowing what she will find.

He lies between two rocks, his body mangled and torn. He has crawled here out of instinct but can go no further. His remaining eye is gone, plucked by the tiger. Blind as he is, even were he able to move, he'd soon be dead.

She steps closer. His face stares lifelessly up. He has fought for her; now he will fight no more. She licks his face, nuzzles his empty eyes, breathes upon his bloodied mask.

Across the field the fool collects his stones and moves toward town, taking with him all the stars. The sky begins to lighten.

She stays till dawn.

THE GARDEN LIES DAZED in the morning sun. On a tree branch above, a single thrush chatters loudly as if to burst. Near the base of the wall the cat appears through a curtain of ivy and leaf. Her steps are slow, weary. The journey back has been haunted by ghosts, flickering, unreachable, taunting. Again and again she has spun in circles to confront them, dancing on two legs, paws flailing; then fled in fear across the piazza, seeking home, the window ledge on which to curl up, a reassuring voice from the kitchen, the comfort of hands.

But the house is quiet. The schoolteacher who lives here has left for work. The cat sits on her haunches, feeling the seed taking hold inside her, a reward for her reckless fecundity. Once again she will carry the past in her womb, bear a nest of mewling sorrows. Despite her speed, her exquisite balance, the graceful arc of her leap, she is no better off than the dogs she despises, in chains to forces she cannot overcome. Her contempt, which has been her power, is for the moment gone. Now in her weakness she craves kindness.

On the porch steps sits a saucer of milk.

She approaches, cautiously. Her stomach rumbles; the milk smells sweet. Tucking her front paws under, she surrenders, and laps. Instantly there is relief. With the milk comes a surge of well-being, of strength, renewal, power. She will drink her fill, then jump to the window and nap in the morning sun, regaining her force, shedding the past. Tonight, restored, she will hunt.

Here, cat.

Someone is in the garden.

Here, cat.

She knows this young man, who comes to the house in the afternoons to visit the schoolteacher.

Come here cat.

His voice is soothing, reassuring.

Here, cat.

He reaches down. In his hand is a length of twine. In spite of herself, she purrs.

Here.

In the branches above the thrush trumpets a joyous hosannah.

THE LEGEND

D own a dusty lane and then another, where the noise of the Piazza grew faint and quiet filled the July air, there stood a high wall of ancient stones next to which the cypress trees grew tall. Late afternoons young boys, among them Niccolò, perched in the branches like monkeys, imbibing the cool emanations that rose from the gardens within. This place was different from all other places in the world. This was the Convent Figlie del Sacro Cuore di Gesù. Nuns lived here.

More to the point, behind these walls walked the most beautiful woman on earth.

As to the nuns, there were things the boys knew, even at their young age, about the Sisters of the Lamb of God. For one, they had beards of coarse hair and wore barbed wire beneath their robes to protect their privates from *succubi*. Reports had surfaced of unbaptized babies devoured alive in dark midnight rituals, though this was not classified as fact. One truth, however, was indisputable: there was, living among them, a ward, a goddess; a living embodiment of that beauty which God once intended for all women, but for reasons unknown was denied to most.

Her name was Vittoria Bianca Apollonia de Patrizia. On Piazza Santa Caterina Piccola, she was royalty.

Who she was, where she came from, the specifics of her past were well established among the inhabitants of town, depending on who you asked. A Pomeranian princess; a Spanish *hidalga* snatched from her crib by anarchists, nurtured by gypsies, kidnapped by a Moroccan sheik, a child bride at twelve; then a daring escape from a seraglio wrapped in rugs, across perilous seas to the safety of the gates of Sacro Cuore di Gesù. If the precise details of the story did not always match, on one point they converged. Along with the *Principessa* had come a chest, studded with jewels, containing an emperor's gift of diamonds and precious stones that lay, to this very day, deep in the labyrinths of the nunnery. A dowry worth millions, enshrined in layers of dust.

Despite these rumors of wealth, however, and despite her great beauty, it was her modesty that outshone all else. When, evenings, she appeared on Piazza Piccola for the *passeggiata*, surrounded by a protective entourage of nuns, her soft smiles and gentle glances seemed to confer grace on all she passed. A nod to an elderly matron, a pat on a small child's head; priests and farmers alike became dumbstruck in her presence. Yet for all this she had no suitors. No man dared to take her arm, though some had tried. Over the years one or the other of Piazza Piccola's most daring bachelors had braved the phalanx of nuns surrounding her on her evening walk. Fedoras in hand, knees quaking, they dared to venture into her path.

"*Signorina. Che piacere!*"

One look from her limpid eyes, bluer than blue, flecked with silver, aglow with the light of exotic lands, towering minarets, scented seraglios – one glance and the most ardent suitor fell back, overwhelmed. It was to be expected. Where in this town of farmers and goatherds and blacksmiths would any man worthy of her grandeur arise?

"SHE COULD BE HAD," stated Giovanni Di Cenzo over the clattering of pots in the kitchen of Menucci's Caffè. "If a man had the heart of a lion, the balls of a conqueror, she could be won."

The other busboys guffawed. "And who would that lion be, Giovanni? A peasant like you with sauce on his apron?"

Fire rose in Giovanni's cheeks. "Measure a man not by his rags, but by his aspirations! In that lies his greatness!"

"In that case," sneered Rocco, the head cook, holding out a mop, "I suggest you aspire to wipe the floor."

"Gutless fools," spat Giovanni.

They hooted and drifted away, all but Giulio Massimo, the dishwasher, who was amused by his friend's hot-headed pronouncements.

"If you feel so strongly, why not inform the *Principessa* of your passions? She's certain to be impressed."

"Me, the son of a pot-seller from Urbino?" growled Giovanni, leaning on the mop. "She wouldn't look at me twice. Only true greatness could woo her; a man who had sacrificed everything, given up all that was dear for glory and fame. A hero in whose shining presence she might feel at last an equal partner."

Now even Giulio laughed. "Then slink away now, *amico*. That man none of us will ever be."

"Speak for yourself," was Giovanni's response.

L'amore vince tutto: a heart on fire scorns defeat. But aspire as Giovanni might to become something more than God and nature had made him, heroes are heroes and busboys are not. Night after night he stood in the shadows, frozen with passion and shame, unable to speak as the *Principessa* passed by aloof to his existence.

So, finally, slink away is what Giovanni Di Cenzo did. Stung by the ridicule of his friends, choked by a passion without requite, one day he was gone from the town of Monte Castella. This, however, had happened some years before Niccolò was born. No one remembered the smitten busboy. Why would they? The son of a pot seller had disappeared. Life went on. Years passed, not without events; on the piazza events were like mice, one in every pantry. As for the *Principessa*, her beauty and legend only grew. Weekends she attended the cinema where, as her eyes rose to the screen, the rest of the theater watched her watching Valentino play the Sheik. All agreed they made a perfect pair. But Valentino, like *Il Duce*, was far away in Hollywood, while Vittoria Bianca Apollonia de Patrizia lived, breathed, and walked on Piazza Piccola.

And in every man's dreams.

FAUSTO SAW THEM FIRST, approaching through shimmering waves of July heat: the horse, magnificent, fierce; the rider, imperious, erect, helmet spiked and plumed. One sleeve hung empty; across one eye stretched a silken patch. His medals flashed in the sun.

Fausto whistled to the Widow Petacci at the well, who dropped her washing and elbowed the young Signora Chiusi, who looked, then blushed and crossed herself twice. Past Scarpacci's butcher shop, past the *caffè*, past Morelli's fruit cart where Morelli and his horse sat dozing in the midday heat, past the bakery where Niccolò helped sweep the floors, horse and rider continued in regal procession to the entrance of the Grand Hotel Imperiale. Such was the nature of Piazza Santa Caterina Piccola that by the time the stranger had dismounted his horse and been shown to his suite of rooms high up beneath the majestic hotel flags, everyone in town knew of his arrival. And such was the nature of Piazza Piccola that everyone immediately had an opinion.

"Prussian," stated Boldoni the pharmacist. "Hohenzollern."

"Austrian," surmised Biggio the barber, expert in all things to do with war. "Uhlan."

"More likely Chevaux Legers," suggested Barzini the ice man, seated in Biggio's barber chair. A heated argument ensued, which resulted in loud threats and a slightly nicked ear.

Even Mamma took time to look from the window of the bakery where Niccolò was helping to sort the raisins. But she offered no opinion.

An answer was not long in coming. "His name," reported the Widow Petacci, who was in charge of all pertinent local rumors and who had heard it from Ricardo Ignacci, the maître d' at the hotel, who had stolen a glance at the guestbook and therefore was in a position to know, "is *Generalissimo*

Maggiore Arturo D'Ambrosio, formerly of His Majesty's cavalry. A decorated hero. A personal friend of the Duce."

Everyone felt vindicated. All but Giulio Massimo, the former dishwasher at Menucci's *Caffè* who over the years had ascended to the exalted position of waiter. He watched with interest as the Generalissimo paraded past the *caffè* at noon; noted the empty sleeve, the patch on one eye. But if Giulio had thoughts about the event, he kept his mouth shut.

For one full day no more was seen of the General. This lack of solid information served as fertile ground for unfounded rumors. What was the reason for this perplexing visitation? Was something bigger in the air - a visit, say, from the *Duce* himself?

"A possibility," mused the Widow Petacci.

"*Cazzate*," spat Nonno. "*Duce*? Why would that horse's ass bother with this meaningless pizzle of a town?"

The suspense was ended a day later when the General appeared at the hotel entrance, in full regalia, and set out across the Piazza, his movements telegraphed by a host of watching eyes, so that when he arrived at Menucci's *Caffè* a table had already been prepared.

"*Generalissimo!*" shouted Menucci at the top of his lungs. "I am honored!"

"The honor, sir, is mine," nodded the bemedaled visitor.

"*Vino!*" bellowed Minucci. "My finest!"

In seconds the General sat sipping a glass of Menucci's most expensive chianti and gazing onto Piazza Piccola, a dubious vista at best. But word was out: in no time arrived a welcoming committee of Monte Castella's most honored citizens, whose broad smiles and hearty handshakes made it clear that they had come for an inquisition.

A larger table was laid. More wine was poured. Before the interrogation could begin Generalissimo Arturo D'Ambrosio held up a single, gloved hand – his only hand, as it happened.

"I sense you have questions, sirs. Therefore, allow to me present myself, and my reasons for being here, for I have travelled a great distance to find your enchanting town, and I would be pleased to make a good impression."

This was acceptable to the Committee as well as to the small crowd gathering on the sidewalk outside the *caffè*.

"My story," the Generalissimo continued, "is simple. I am a soldier. The points of my compass are Duty, Honor, Battle, Victory. In my career I have commanded armies, conquered empires, met and defied the foe in foreign lands: Turks, Arabs, dervishes and almond-eyed Chinamen. I have seen brave men fall, beloved heroes lost. I have bathed in the blood of slaughter on African shores. I have sacrificed arm and eye in His Majesty's name, without regrets. Never have I tasted dishonor. But now..."

At this, he leaned forward.

"...the time has come to lay down the sword, relinquish my command. The time for war is over. I have, I admit humbly, amassed certain wealth. And so I have searched for the right place to live out my days in peace." He gestured, taking in the entire piazza in a single sweep of his arm. "*Ecco.* The moment I laid eyes on your peaceful town, I knew I had found the object of my quest."

He sat back and sipped his wine. In the silence, the Committee considered his words. It was left to Biggio the barber to formulate the question on everyone's mind.

"Why here?"

The Generalissimo set down his glass and smiled.

"Why not?" he said.

And that was that. His story told, the Generalissimo ordered a banquet of food and wine for all assembled. There was laughter and great good humor. Everyone was pleased; except for one. As waiters bustled around the tables, refilling glasses, setting down plates, one waiter, Giulio in fact, leaned down to whisper in the Generalissimo's ear.

"Giovanni. What the fuck are you doing?"

To which the Generalissimo half-turned to Giulio as if he might have misheard. "*Scusi?*"

"In God's name, what's happened to you? Your eye? Your arm?"

The Generalissimo frowned. "It would seem, sir, you have confused me with another man."

"Is there a problem?" called Menucci from across the table.

"Of course not," replied the Generalissimo, with a nod to Giulio. "Simply a case of mistaken identity."

But Giulio's hand had already reached out, already found its way to the silk patch covering the Generalissimo's eye. There were gasps around the table, then shouts of angry alarm. "Stop that fool!" A forest of rough hands pulled Giulio away, preparing to pummel him onto the floor.

"Stop! *Basta!*" boomed the Generalissimo. "Leave that man!" The power of his command reminded some of the great *Generale* Antonio Baldissera, whose armies freed the beleaguered garrisons of Cassale and put to rout the forces of King Menelek II nearly a century before.

Immediately Giulio was unhanded. "He meant no harm," smiled the Generalissimo. "Simple curiosity." Then, to Giulio, "I only hope you found what you were looking for."

And with that, the matter was dropped. The celebration resumed; while later, alone in the kitchen, Giulio drank an entire bottle of wine, shaken by what he had seen.

NEWS OF *Generalissimo* Arturo D'Ambrosio's plans – every detail – raced across the square, accruing nuance and inspiration with each telling; then back in the other direction, polished, gilt-edged, and engraved, so that by evening the story had acquired the smooth patina of infallible legend. Whether by chance, error, or destiny, Piazza Piccola had at long last a superior personage in its midst. It was instantly a matter of civic pride, and why not? That a man of his stature would find delight in the particular ambience of Monte Castella was not really so surprising; charm was a matter of taste. Already, there was talk of a statue.

And, inevitably, there came an epiphany.

Wherever the thought was first expressed; in Biggio's barbershop; over candlelight at the *caffè*; possibly from the Widow Petacci herself, once released the idea took wing, until everyone claimed it as their own. As days went by the idea began to seem undeniable: at last, Piazza Santa Caterina Piccola had discovered a worthy suitor for the Madonna of the convent. Fate had sent the Generalissimo for Vittoria Bianca Apollonia de Patrizia. Fate would bring them together. It was just a matter of time.

The time, as it happened, arrived on a sultry summer night, under a luminous moon, not three days after the *Generalissimo's* providential appearance. Perhaps it was the soft breezes, carrying whispers of far-off Mediterranean gardens, that prompted Vittoria Bianca Apollonia to join the *passeggiata*; perhaps it was something more. Whatever the reason, promptly at seven in the evening she entered the Piazza accompanied by the usual contingent of nuns.

Her appearance had been anticipated.

A host of eyes watched as the she moved beneath the glowing streetlamps, smiling at the displays in the lighted shop windows. Across the square beneath the awning of the Hotel Imperiale the Generalissimo, imposing in tunic and medals, emerged from the shadows and strode majestically in the opposite direction. Like pieces in a magnificent chess game, warrior and empress closed the distance between them, each unaware of the other's presence on the board.

What might happen when they met – or whether they might meet at all – was an outcome too problematical for the citizenry of Piazza Piccola; some things, it had been agreed, were best not left to chance. Which was why at that critical moment, as *Generalissimo* and *Principessa* approached a rendezvous in front of the glowing windows of Boldoni's Farmacia, as if by divine intervention, Valentino Umberti, known as "the sheik" for his elegant suits and rakish fedora (though everyone knew by day he shoveled manure at the stables) stepped forward into the gap between them.

"*Piacere,*" he bowed, "If I may, allow me to effect an introduction."

What followed was witnessed by no less than a score of onlookers: the curious, fluttering glance upward by Vittoria Bianca Apollonia as, with a commanding step forward, the Generalissimo presented himself, shoulders squared, medals gleaming, for her inspection; his crisp military bow, saber carefully swept to one side; her response, raven hair stirring in the soft breeze, full lips briefly parting ("Oh," they seemed to say), the fluttering rise of her bosom; then his charge, a bold step forward against the battle line of nuns escorting her, whereupon the escort fell back, leaving their flagship vulnerable and exposed.

It was a brilliant tactic, *a coup de main*. Into the breach of her acquiescence stepped the Generalissimo. Victory certain, he offered his arm.

"May I have the distinct pleasure of escorting the Signorina across the Piazza?" he said.

With only a moment's pause, she reached for his elbow and surrendered. The couple moved down the walk; behind them the wreckage of the armada of nuns could do nothing but drift helplessly in the backwash.

It is generally recalled that at that moment, as if by design, the bells in the steeple of St. Bartolomeo begin to chime the hour, an hour that would not soon be forgotten.

⌒

THE DAYS THAT FOLLOWED brought a new spirit to the piazza, a sense of lightness and anticipation that mixed with the noise of wagons and the smell of sheep and manure. By day the mundane labors of life went on, but when evening arrived few were immune to the latest news regarding the Generalissimo and Vittoria Bianca Apollonia. Their soiree had become a spectator event, every smile, every tilt of the head catalogued and recorded in the journal of public hearsay. To this had been added a nightly repair to the newly renamed *Duce* Dining Room of the Grand Hotel Imperiale where, protected from prying eyes, a sumptuous table was laid. Here the illustrious couple supped and conversed – he, eye glittering, mustache perfectly waxed, relating tales of triumphs, of breakneck charges, heroic deeds, the battle to the death with the Aga of Turkistan, in which an arm was lost; and she, perfect in eyes and lips, head thrown back in a sumptuous laugh, growing more perfect with each moment as if time were her friend, intent on making her younger by the hour. It was clear what they felt, two shipwrecked strangers washed up on an unexpected shore to find the love they'd waited for all their lives.

129

The movies were nothing compared to this.

While outside in the streets and alleys of Piazza Piccola, amid the drab and mind-numbing work of merchants and farmers and pigs and children, an ember of hope was rekindled. People smiled. Mamma danced a *trescone*, all by herself, one night while Niccolò said his prayers.

Only Giulio, the waiter, reserved judgment.

Still. he kept his mouth shut.

TWO WEEKS went by. From Rome came new pronouncements to which, as usual, no one paid attention. Affairs of state could wait; more important matters were afoot. In the *caffè*, around the well, in the shops the affairs of *Princessa* and *Generalissimo* were discussed more than the weather. Naturally, people began to yearn for the next development, the logical evolution of the story: the proposal, the acceptance; the wedding.

"*Magnifico!*" imagined the ladies at the well. "The Cardinal himself will come to bless the bride." At the barber shop the men debated: was it possible the *Duce* himself would make time to attend? It never occurred to anyone the event would happen anywhere else. Clearly, history had reserved Piazza San Caterina Piccola for this event.

There followed more sober concerns. Once the banns had been published there would surely be visitors. From Rome, certainly, governors and smartly-dressed *fascisti*, impressive motorcars, stylish ingenues in the latest Paris fashions; from far-flung military outposts in Europe and Africa, the cream of military splendor. All would have needs; all would have money to spend. Without doubt it would be the most glittering assemblage of social elite to walk the sidewalks of Piazza Piccola. The place would need sprucing up.

("Let 'em walk in the dung," huffed Nonno. "We do.")

Then finally, news, this time from the tailor, who had been summoned to the *Generale's* rooms to repair a flaw in the *Generalissimo's* epaulets. The facts were this: at the Generalissimo's request a formal invitation had been issued by the Sisters of the Lamb of God for supper at the Convent Figlie del Sacro Cuore di Gesù on the evening of Tuesday next. It was the first time in memory such an invitation had been extended to a member of the laity.

There could be no doubt as to its import, or to the Generalissimo's intentions: to storm the castle and secure a blessing for his proposal of marriage. Nor was there any doubt the nuns would agree. The gates of the temple would open, the beautiful prisoner inside would be freed. And when the evening arrived, bringing with it yet another luminous moon, who could doubt that all would be well?

At the appointed hour, then, the Generalissimo, resplendent in white, arrived at the convent gate on horseback and was admitted. Behind him the gates closed. With that a vigil began, the only clues to the evening's progress coming from spies perched in the trees overlooking the walls while within, destiny played her hand.

Seven o'clock came and went, as did eight, with no news. Children were fed and put to bed. Just after nine, lanterns were spotted in the hallways of the upper floors of the convent. Not long afterward, candlelight flickered from windows tucked high under the gabled roof where, it was rumored, the *Principessa* kept her silk-and-scented apartments. At nine-thirty Quindici, the stonecutter's son, who had managed to bring along his father's flask full of brandy, lost his balance, slipped from his branch and fell with a crash into a hay wagon parked below; the cries of distress that followed had more to do with his father's blows than bruises from the fall.

Then at ten voices were heard in the convent courtyard. The gates of the nunnery opened. The Generalissimo, regal as ever, guided his horse out onto the cobblestones and up the lane toward the piazza, past the *caffè* where his dream had first been expressed: past the *farmacia*, the bakery, to the hotel entrance, where he dismounted. He strode through the lobby without a word and up the stairs to his rooms.

At the convent the flickering light in the window beneath the gables was extinguished. In the darkness the small town seemed to hold its breath. The fires were banked. The moon set. But no one slept. All over town, in the bedrooms of young women, perhaps young men as well, possibilities hovered like sugarplums. Stars fairy-danced in the deep magenta sky. The drowsy world seemed to float in a state of grace.

Then came the crack of a gunshot.

Shortly after, anguished screams. There were cries for a doctor, a fury of desperate comings and goings in the Grand Hotel Imperiale. The switchboard was flooded with calls. Confusion reigned, but by dawn, the truth was manifest. Generalissimo Maggiore Arturo D'Ambrosio, formerly of His Majesty's cavalry, a decorated hero, a personal friend of *Il Duce*, was dead by his own hand.

Three days later the Generalissimo was buried in the Cimitero Monumentale of Monte Castella. Of the many dignitaries in Rome and across the far-flung colonies of the empire who were expected, not one came.

THEORIES EMERGED. Had the Generalissimo's death been an unfortunate accident? Or worse, a murder, cleverly disguised? Accounts circulated of sinister sightings on the night of the death – strangers in cloaks, veiled assassins. None were confirmed. There was, in addition, the letter from Rome, which stated that, sorry to say, neither the Duce nor anyone in the Government had heard of Generalissimo Maggiore Arturo D'Ambrosio. This, however, served to prove nothing: those very denials, it was suggested, simply underlined the importance of the man. Besides, the very idea that the citizenry of Monte Castella could have been mistaken in their estimation of the man was preposterous. So, like all news from Rome, this was ignored.

Certainly the *Principessa* Vittoria Bianca Apollonia de Patrizia could not be blamed, though for a great while she remained behind doors. Her grief was assumed, her absence from the *passeggiata* appropriate. Eventually, suspicion fell on the Sisters of the Lamb of God. Was it possible they had refused the marriage? Was it jealousy that motivated them? Revenge for the Generalissimo's daring? Or was it just the poisonous bile of their own unhappiness, the result of lives spent in barren denial, that led them to deny the bliss of marriage to the woman they called their own?

In the heat of the moment, questions were asked, counsel taken, answers demanded. When after some months, however, none were forthcoming, the furor began to subside. The mundane labors of daily life went on. And although there had been a great loss, the *Principessa* still lived, still lifted her limpid eyes to the cinema screen. Perhaps, then, it was better just to be content with the shining grace of her presence. Perhaps if beauty like hers could not belong to one man, it was enough it belonged to everyone.

So people began to forget.

Except for one man, Giulio Massimo.

It was he alone who had questioned the Generalissimo's story; he who had peeked beneath the distinguished eye patch. It was Giulio who received the letter that had been dropped in the postbox of the Grand Hotel Imperiale on the night of the event, written in the hand of a very old friend.

"My Dear Giulio," it began.

"As to my whereabouts in the years since I left Monte Castella suffice it to say my sole intention was to return not as I had been, but as I had determined to be. The sacrifices required, though in some cases unspeakably painful, were nothing compared to the prize: to secure as my own, forever, the grace and affections of Vittoria Bianca Apollonia Antonia de Patrizia. And even if in time she were to discover my masquerade, my lack of title and wealth, surely by then these things would amount to nothing compared to the truth of my heart and the depth of my passion. Surely if God were just, true love would prevail."

The letter went on, the story unfolded: how, passing through the convent gates that evening, Giovanni Di Cenzo, son of a pot maker, felt his dream at last in his grasp. How, once tea had been poured and pleasantries exchanged, when the "Generalissimo" stood to voice his proposal of marriage, quite suddenly Vittoria Bianca rose from her chair. Before he continued, she said, she wished to impart to him certain information, upon which his proposal might hinge. Would he care to repair to her rooms?

"Puzzled, I followed her by candlelight up dark stairways and down silent hallways, untrodden by men for decades, if not centuries. At last we reached her doorway, high under the rafters. She motioned me to enter. I did. And here, my great shock began."

"Her dwelling consisted of a single room, a meager cell. Instead of divans of silks and satins, my eye beheld only a simple bed and a hard wooden chair. In place of brocaded gowns and pillows, a rough cloth robe.

No balms or perfumes, no scented candles, no vanities of marble and gold. A rude washbowl of wood. Nothing more."

"She directed my gaze toward one corner in which stood, not a bejeweled chest, but a rudely-hewn cradle; filled not with precious stones, but with dust and cobwebs and a small, tattered blanket. "

"Only now, having brought me to this place, did she summon the courage to explain."

"'You see before you the inheritance of an orphan,' she said. 'The blanket which swaddled me at birth, in which I was left years ago at this convent gate. Never, despite all which is rumored, have I lived elsewhere. I possess neither wealth nor title; my adventures are small. I am, I fear, nothing more than a poor country girl. This now I confess.'"

"In the flickering light of the candle, she blushed. Her eyes had filled with shame and regret."

"'So you see,' she continued, 'What people have made of me is only what they wished to see. I am their figment, the page on which they write their wishes. My hope is that, knowing this, you can forgive and let love prevail. I leave in your hands what to do next.'"

"With that she fixed me with a look of such longing I thought my heart might melt. Indeed, for a better man, a nobler soul, that look alone would have been worth the price."

"But too late. My heart had frozen. The scales had fallen from my eyes. The truth was suddenly obvious: I, the liar, had been betrayed; my dreams had proven dust, my hopes a mirage."

There was nothing more to say. In an instant, as Vittoria Bianca Apollonia became nothing more than a rude peasant girl, so too did Generalissimo Maggiore Arturo D'Ambrosio become nothing more than Giovanni Di Cenza, former busboy - even less, by the weight of one eye and one arm. Less even than that, for stripped of his horse, his medals, stripped of his fondest illusions, the man was nothing more than a charade, a ridiculous farce played out for an audience of none. His fantastic attempt – brave and heroic as it had been – had come to nothing.

So he left.

"I enclose the last of my money. Distribute it as you will. As for the horse and tunic, be kind enough to return them to the man from whom they were borrowed. Anything else I own you may scatter to the winds."

"My best, Giovanni."

True to his friendship, Giulio returned the horse and tunic, and put the money in the Church box for the poor. The letter he burned.

As for the rest, he kept his mouth shut.

THERE REMAINS the matter of the truth, if truth has any place in this story. Consider Vittoria Bianca Apollonia de Patrizia in the days that followed the death of her suitor, reclining on her bed of silken pillows as around her the nuns scurry to replace the meaningless cradle of wood with her magnificent chest overflowing with jewels.

Consider her sorrow at having unmasked the one man she might have loved.

Consider her pique at finding this silly, yet mildly diverting game at an end.

Consider her impatience as the interminable years of pampered imprisonment stretch before her.

Does she ache for her life lost, a world of palaces and seraglios, epic battles on darkling plains?

Or is she, in fact, who she said she was – a simple peasant girl?

Chissa. There is no knowing.

LO SCALPELLINO

Only after he had travelled to the four points of the compass, testing the limits of his courage and manhood, did young Adamo Ragonese return to his father's monument yard across from the cemetery near Piazza Piccola, having been struck dumb by gas and bombardment in the Battle of Caporetto in 1915. Being speechless, he spoke to no one about things he had seen. He set down his rucksack, hugged his father, picked up a chisel and set to work carving headstones for sale to the recently bereaved.

Unlike the magnificent statuary that stood in the front of the yard – heroic shapes in granite and marble, saints and cherubs and angels, eyes raised to the glory of Heaven – the stones Adamo carved were spare and simple, unadorned by piety. Into each slab of fieldstone went poetry and truth; intimate, evocative and fair. One might catch in the swirls of each design a glimpse of hopes undone, bright futures diminished, noble souls at rest.

Viewed more closely, though, at certain angles and in certain kinds of light, other truths emerged: Gallipoli, Verdun, the Somme. Orders botched, messages unreceived, mounted officers with donkey's heads sipping schnapps while soldiers no more than boys fell butchered and gassed.

No one, thought Adamo's father, would want such things. He made preparations to sell them for scrap.

To his surprise, however, the first stone was purchased within days; as was the next and the one after that. As fast as Adamo carved them, sometimes one or two in a week, the stones were paid for and carried away. News of their exquisite beauty quickly spread; within months the yard was besieged with collectors, some from as far away as Rome, intent on acquiring an authentic Ragonese headstone, price being no object when it came to Eternity, or for that matter Art.

As his fortunes prospered, Adamo's father considered expanding his yard, even moving it to a larger *cimitero* in a more exclusive location. Then one afternoon Adamo set down his chisel and spoke, his voice rusty through years of disuse.

"*Finito*," he said.

He picked up his rucksack, hugged his father and left, having said what he had to say.

The stone yard stayed where it was.

CONTRAPPUNTO

Hartory, chronicler of mankind's fondest hopes and greatest follies, had scrawled her name only lightly upon the hill town of Monte Castella. Whether due to the composition of the water, or the ratio of sheep to artists, or perhaps the altitude, something in the character of the place formed a natural barrier against change. Centuries of invaders from all points of the compass had hauled their catapults and battering rams up the steep mountain road to this preposterous outcropping of a village only to find it, once conquered, stolidly unconquerable. Realizing this they lingered long enough to execute a few inhabitants, build a few walls and drop a few crumbs of culture before packing up and heading to more fruitful prospects for war, rape and pillage below.

The place, it seemed, was impregnable. Even with the advent of newer roads, electric lights, telephones and a postal system, the town remained aloof from the tides of politics and social engineering. Though great events might occur in the cities below - jackboots on the streets of Rome, books ordered burned, slogans to be memorized - never mind; in a country where nothing is allowed but everything is permitted these minor disturbances, it was assumed, would in time melt away like a dusting of snow in tomorrow's warmth.

Still, a determined invader will seek a way, and the new century had brought to mankind a new invader, impervious to distance, blockade, good taste or art. Like the Trojan horse at the gates of Ilium it arrived hidden in plain sight; in this case in the back room of Bruno Fabbro's Quality Livery and Stables, across from and upwind of Menucci's Caffè on Piazza Santa Caterina Piccolo.

Bruno Fabbro, barely five feet tall in his heavily manured boots and sporting a mustache seemingly half as long as his height, was known to his neighbors as a quarrelsome soul. He spent his mornings in the entrance to his establishment conducting business with the ferocity of a man who loved money, tolerated horses and hated people. He trusted no one, the sole exception being a man he'd never met but admired with a fervor bordering on adoration - namely *Il Duce*, Benito Mussolini. To Bruno the Iron Prefect, Prime Minister of Rome, and swaggering leader of the Italian *fascisti* movement represented all that was admirable in *uomo moderno*: firmness, resolve, bellicosity, and strength. And while the circumstances of geography – Rome being far from Monte Castella – hardly afforded him the opportunity to share a table with the Great Man himself, Bruno possessed the next best thing; a GE All-Mahogany Model-S22X radio, his prized possession, acquired years before in a canny if dubious trade for an asthmatic and slightly swayback drayhorse.

It wasn't a fancy radio. The reception, Monte Castella being surrounded by mountains, was not always ideal. Still each day after lunch, as the rest of the shops along the piazza shut their doors for the traditional afternoon *riposo*, Bruno (whose wife forbade him to come home without first removing his boots) retired to his desk in the tack room, tuned the dial to station EIAR and sat back to hear his idol's voice broadcasting directly from Rome.

And what a voice it was, even filtered through a haze of static. Commanding, guttural, belligerent, haughty, disdainful, pompous, overbearing; a voice that commanded respect in some, trepidation in others, but for Bruno a devotion bordering on worship. Although the specific concepts of the Duce's political philosophy may at times have been foggy in his head - socialism being hardly commensurate with the horse-trading business - the fervor of his sayings, delivered with thundering vehemence, were enough to inspire Bruno to tune in each day. And why not? If a man chose to spend a part of every afternoon with his ear to the radio, what harm was there in that? *A ciascuno il suno* - to each his own.

Besides, it was only a small radio. If Bruno Fabbro wanted to listen, no problem.

Almost no problem.

Directly across from Bruno's stables, above Menucci's Caffè, behind a door festooned with posted bills and yellowing invoices, lived Cesario Dell Aqualina De Cortona, aesthete, epicurean, gentle aristocrat. Heir to a noble family dating back centuries but in recent generations fallen on more austere times, Cesario wore his title as he did his slightly yellowed white suit, with the dignity commensurate to a faded *cavaliere*. With his pencil-thin mustache, graying temples and air of sophisticated nonchalance he stood as a symbol of a more genteel and elegant way of life, a time before men of his breeding owed everyone money. He hated conflict and avoided bad manners.

But he loved opera.

Verdi, Rossini, Puccini, Wagner; in their towering works could be discerned, Cesario fervently believed, the culmination of human achievement, evidence of the sublime hand of a refined and benevolent Creator. On the rising crescendos of Mozart's *Die Zauberflöte* one might climb a stairway to heaven, or descend to the fires of hell in the maelstrom of Berlioz' *Faust*. And while present circumstances hardly afforded him a box at La Scala in Milan, Cesario did possess the next best thing: a Columbia "Princess" Grafonola Victrola, circa 1912, a castaway of his late great uncle's estate. Its mahogany case and gleaming brass bell were his most treasured possession, a link to his mannerly past, the final remnant of a lost and more graceful age.

Afternoons, when the sun beat down and the clatter of pots and pans from the *caffè* kitchen directly beneath his rooms had subsided, it was Cesario's habit to fling open his windows, set a recording onto the turntable, lower the needle and retire to the luxury of his bathtub where, on his back in a solution of warm salt water and oils, sipping a glass of the finest brandy he could manage on credit, he floated, eyes closed, imagining the gramophone as his own barrel-chested diva while the glories of *Orfeo, La Traviata* and the like drifted across the room, out the windows and across the piazza.

Everyone heard it, the soaring cadenzas of Enrico Caruso, the rapturous *coloratura* of Lily Pons, echoing like choirs of angels in the afternoon heat. Fausto, by his stone hut near the well, would pause in his sweeping of stones to gaze upward, sensing the presence of the eternal. Monsignore Don Federico, tending his garden, would contemplate the tragic arc of *Rigoletto* and find inspiration for next Sunday's sermon. Mamma, dusting sweat and baking flour from her brow, would hearken to *Electra*'s dark revenge and nod, her heart taking wing. Even Nonno would manage a grudging smile. In short, everyone on Piazza Santa Caterina Piccolo enjoyed the music wafting from Cesario Dell Aqualina De Cortona's window.

Everyone but Bruno Fabbro.

To Bruno, whose musical tastes tended toward marching bands and circus calliopes, opera was annoying enough, on a par with the agonized mooing of unmilked cows. When it interrupted the *Duce's* daily broadcasts, however, it became more than mere annoyance. The fact was his small radio could hardly compete with the lungs of the great baritones and mezza-sopranos whose impassioned howlings descended upon him each day from across the piazza, burying the Duce's latest pronouncements beneath an avalanche of thundering *sfortzando*. Surely, Bruno grumbled to himself, the mighty tenets of fascism deserved at least an equal hearing in the public square.

With that in mind one afternoon when a particularly compelling tirade from *Il Duce* was interrupted by a burst of shrieking *arioso* from Cesario's window, Bruno determined to deal with the problem as any good neighbor might. Taking pen in hand he composed a message, crossed the piazza to Menucci's Caffè and climbed the stairs to Cesario's apartment where, finding a space among the clutter of previously posted notices of overdue payment, he pinned the note to Cesario's door:

Stai zitta la chiasso. Fabbro.

Stop the noise.

Having done so he returned to his livery, confident the situation would find itself resolved in a reasonable and neighborly way. Imagine his dismay when the following afternoon, at the very moment the Iron Prefect launched into an attack on the foundations of capitalism, the air was shattered by the lovesick cries of the doomed Ethiopian princess *Aida*, dying noisily in her lover's arms. Unmoved by the pathos of her tragic dilemma and annoyed to find a situation that had seemed resolved quite obviously not, Bruno considered his options. Fortunately, at that moment a course of action presented itself in the *Duce*'s own words, providentially audible through the static:

"Better to live a day as a lion than one hundred years as a sheep."

Thus inspired, Bruno again crossed the piazza, ascended the stairs to Cesario's apartments and knocked on the door, this time prepared to state his case more forcefully. After some delay the door opened, revealing Cesario in his silk bathrobe, having been roused from the dreamy warmth of his tub.

"*Sì?*" smiled Cesario, having no idea who the fellow at his door might be.

"Did you read my message?" growled Bruno, coming right to the point.

"What message?" frowned Cesario.

Bruno pointed. *"Ecco,"* he remarked, feeling no need to elaborate on what had already been written.

Cesario glanced at the door, seeing only the forest of overdue bills. "As it happens," he replied "I find myself at present short of funds. Come back next month." He moved to shut the door.

Bruno's boot was already in it.

"Not the bills," he announced. To avoid further confusion, he pulled the note from the door and held it up:

Stop the noise. Fabbro.

Cesario peered at it. "Noise? What noise?"

From the front room came a burst of robust *bel canto* from the lungs of the irrepressible Claudia Muzio.

"That noise," said Bruno.

"That's not noise," explained Cesario. "That's Puccini."

Bruno stood unmoved, wondering if perhaps he'd been insulted. Only then did Cesario recognize the diminutive and mustachioed fellow in front of him as the owner of the stables across the street.

"Perhaps," he suggested, striking a note of neighborly consideration, "you'd prefer something different. Mascagni, for instance. *Cavalliera Rusticana?*" Smiling, he adjusted the belt of his kimono. "It has horses."

"I wish to die in your arms!" bellowed Aida from the front room.

At that moment, had Bruno been a more patient man; had Cesario not sensed his bath growing cold; had not the Ethiopian princess chosen that moment to attempt an F above high C, a reasonable dialogue might have ensued, culminating in an agreement amenable to both sides. Bruno Fabbro, however, was not a man of patience, nor was **Cesario Dell Aqualina De Cortona** inclined to accept the opinions of a mere stable keep whose shoes, reeking of manure, were at present blocking his doorway. In place of further discussion, then, Bruno stepped forward and jabbed his finger into Cesario's chest.

"Stop the music," he growled.

"Absolutely not," replied Cesario.

"*Idiota,*" snarled Bruno.

"*Buffone,*" sniffed Cesario.

"The fatal stone now closes over me," bellowed Aida.

With that Bruno returned to his stables, Cesario to his bath, Aida to her tomb, Mussolini to his oratory, and the discussion came to an end.

But not the problem.

WEEKENDS were a busy time for business at Fabbro's Quality Stables and Livery, so it struck some as odd when Bruno shuttered his doors on Friday and rode out of town. Rumors quickly arose, each one less reliable than the last. He'd visited a long-lost cousin in Athens; left his wife for a new bride in Milan; hopped a steamer to Cyprus one step ahead of the police. Those rumors were put to rest on Sunday afternoon when he returned, carrying in his wagon a large wooden crate. A small crowd of curious bystanders stood by to offer advice as the mystery object was jockeyed into the back room of the stables where, with no lack of ceremony, Bruno took crowbar to carton and unveiled its contents: a 1933 **Phillips 834A Super Inductance Bakelite Radio,** the latest and most advanced of its kind.

Impressive it was, both in size – it took up a good part of the tack room, dwarfing its small and suddenly obsolescent predecessor – and more importantly, volume. The moment Bruno flicked the switch on the console the speakers inside the filigreed cabinet roared to life, setting the small knot of observers back on their heels. The reception was clear, without static or interference, undiminished by distance or geography.

"Now," said Bruno, stepping back, crowbar in hand, "We shall see."

He turned a knob: out leapt the *Duce's* voice. Like a tiger unleashed it barged through the stables, burst through the doors and raced across the piazza, gaining power and heft until, with an ominous roar, it flung itself through the open windows of Cesario's apartment.

Needless to say, Cesario, floating blissfully in his tub, reacted with some dismay. Wrapping himself in a towel he stepped to his window in time to see Bruno Fabbro appear in the doorway of the livery - chin raised, arms folded, jaw set defiantly, in the manner of *Duce* himself – as the voice from the radio announced itself as the new presence in town.

"Believe.

Obey.

Fight!"

IT TOOK only minutes for Cesario, impeccably groomed and topped by his finest fedora, to arrive at the stables and carefully pick his way past the stalls to the back room, where Bruno lounged comfortably in his chair as the opening strains of the *Giovinezza*, the *Duce's* favorite anthem, boomed from the radio.

"My congratulations," began Cesario with an overly courteous bow, "on your new acquisition."

Bruno appeared not to hear. From the radio came sounds of raucous cheering and wild applause, loud enough to make conversation difficult.

"Perhaps, however," Cesario continued, unsure of whether Bruno was listening at all, "One might consider–"

From the radio came Mussolini's voice.

"A revolutionist is born, not made!"

Bruno nodded sagely. The applause continued.

"Which is to say –" continued Cesario.

"Inactivity is death!" bellowed the Iron Prefect. In the adjoining stalls several horses snorted and kicked; a shower of hay drifted down from the loft. It occurred to Cesario that in the days of his forebearers such insolence from a lowly groom of the stables might have resulted in hanging or beheading. Nevertheless -

"A meeting of minds," he said, raising his voice above the din. "Might prove –"

"Silence is the only answer you should give to the fools," barked Mussolini.

Sensing the moment for compromise slipping way, Cesario stepped between the radio and Bruno.

"I must," he announced in a voice rich with ancient and noble indignity, "insist!"

Slowly, deliberately, Bruno turned to Cesario and made a gesture well-known in barnyards, stockyards, and brothels all over the world.

After which he stuck out his tongue.

NEGOTIATIONS HAVING FAILED, hostilities commenced. Each afternoon at the appointed hour the engines of combat – in this case a Radiomarelli Argirita Type 33 gramophone and a Phillips 834 Super Inductance Bakelite Radio – roared into battle. From the high ground above Menucci's Caffè came the thunder of high Opera – cannonades of cadenzas and *sfortzandos, recitatif* and *crescendo* – only to be met in return by amplified salvos of rhetoric and bellowed grandiloquence - the Duce's latest harangues in Rome - launched from the open doors of Fabbro's Livery. Echoing across the piazza the swooping coloraturas of *Die Zauberflöte* collided with the fascist slogans of National Socialism. In the air above the Grand Hotel Imperiale Wagner's Valkyries wrestled with tenets of *spazio vitale* and fascist *forza collettiva*. In the confusion of sounds reverberating from rooftop to rooftop art and politics intermingled, often producing unexpected duets, merging *Duce's* bellowing *recitatif* with Tristan's plea to the lost Isolde, or casting the Great Leader as the benighted clown Pagliacci himself.

Naturally the noise, coming as it did during the afternoon *riposo*, caused no little comment among the citizenry. Some were annoyed, some entertained. Some shrugged it off as an ordinary neighborly dispute; others placed it in the great national tradition of feud and vendetta, in the manner of the Guelphs and Ghibellines or Montagues and Capulets. **Nonno, at the oven**, shook his head in disgust. "*Ad ogni pazzo piace il suon del su sonaglio,*" he muttered: "Every fool is pleased with his own folly." No one imagined that the war between the muses of culture and the ruffians of the state was anything more than a minor and temporary disruption.

But when after a week the cacophony continued with no sign of abatement, attempts were made by the citizenry to broker a peace. A committee of local worthies led by Biggio the barber made its way up the stairs to Cesario's apartments where, standing in the doorway in his bathrobe and slippers and sipping his brandy, Cesario heard their appeal for an armistice.

Biggio set out his reasons, noting in passing that the ongoing hostilities were affecting the napping habits of some in the community.

Not to mention, added Ferucci, disturbing the local livestock.

Not to mention, added Menucci, disrupting business at the *caffè* below.

To which, after some respectful consideration, Cesario replied.

"Talk to Fabbro," was his answer. "He started it."

He closed the door.

Duly instructed, the committee made its way across the cobblestones to Bruno Fabbro's back room where once again Biggio spelled out the issues, assisted this time by Baldelli the haberdasher, whose wife's canary had suddenly turned sullen and refused to eat. Fabbro, a frequent customer of Biggio's shop, listened carefully, stroking his mustache and frowning thoughtfully before responding.

"Talk to Cortona," he growled. "He started it." After which, it being nearly two o'clock, he turned on his radio, ending any hope of further negotiation.

Having failed to broker a peace, and not wanting their efforts to be seen to have failed, the committee conferred and decided to wait things out in hopes that one or the other of the combatants would tire of the whole business. Instead, as the days and weeks passed with no quarter given, something else happened: people began to accept the afternoon cacophony as a regular fixture of life, not unlike the crowing of roosters at dawn or the clang of the church bells at vespers. Entrenchment, it appeared, had led to stalemate. As in the War to End All Wars twenty years earlier the conflict seemed destined to go on forever, outlasting generations, unavoidable and inexorable.

Then, just as everyone had gotten used to it, it was suddenly over.

That afternoon when Mussolini's daily harangue erupted from the stable entrance not a soul on Piazza San Caterina Piccola paid attention. In Biggio's barbershop a discussion of the tyrannies of marriage proceeded along well-accustomed lines; in bedrooms all around the square the populace drowsed. When some minutes had passed with no rejoinder from the windows above the *caffè*, however, the slightest ripple of concern began to spread: not over what was heard but rather what wasn't. The barbershop discussion drifted into curious silence; people sat up in their beds; in the bakery Nonno cocked his ear and frowned. When another hour had elapsed and still the great prima donnas of the world had failed to so much as clear their throats, unease turned to concern. In the piazza the amplified ramblings of the *Duce* rang unchallenged in the open air. Goats bleated; dogs barked.

By evening it was clear something was amiss.

Once again, a delegation was formed. Led this time by Monsignore Don Federico they made their way up the stairway to Cesario's door, only to find it standing open. After some whispered discussions the delegation entered, wary of what they might find.

What they found was nothing. Nothing disturbed. Nothing overturned. Nothing broken or even chipped. In the bathroom the tub sat empty. In wardrobe hung Cesario's silk bathrobe and slippers. Everything, it seemed, was in place, except for **Cesario**.

And his gramophone.

Neighbors were questioned, inquiries made. No one, it seemed, had seen him go. Rumors arose as to his sudden departure: he'd purchased a bride in Trieste; rushed to the side of an ailing brother in Catania; inherited an island off Corfu. Perhaps, some theorized, he'd simply skipped out on his debts. Nearly everyone had a theory; all but Bruno Fabbro who, when questioned, simply shrugged. *"Buon viaggio,"* he muttered, and turned away.

For some days and weeks the topic of Cesario's disappearance occupied the civic conversation. Surely, it was thought, some word would come, some clue to his absence. But when time passed and none did, interest began to wane. Events interceded: weddings, funerals, more fiats from Rome, ominous rumors of things to come. Around the piazza other radios began to be heard; more and more the air buzzed with the blare of marching bands and the rhetoric of war, unrefined by counterpoint, untempered by grace or melody. People stopped wondering what had become of Cesario and his gramophone. Everyone forgot because, of course, no one knew.

Except everyone knew.

Knew without knowing.

Fausto knew. Late that night from the window of his hut he'd watched the van glide silently into the square; seen the black-shirted figures emerge;

heard the muffled shouts from above the *caffè*. Half-afraid, he'd followed the van down the road past the ruins, to the river that ran outside of town. The van pulled up. In the moonlight something swirled in the currents. The van pulled away.

Fausto knew. But no one asked him.

Perhaps it was better that way. Better to imagine that Cesario Dell Aqualina De Cortona - aesthete, epicurean, aristocrat – had simply grown tired of the tumult. That one evening he'd stepped from his bath and departed, taking his gramophone with him, setting out for a place where art and nuance still mattered, where culture reigned and no one of importance owed anyone money. Perhaps he'd found a better place, floating, eyes closed - though curiously pale - in lazy circles, as the currents carried him, along with the broken pieces of his gramophone, up the stairs to heaven, or down the river to Valhalla.

In any event, two months later Bruno Fabbro traded his Phillips 834A Super Inductance Bakelite Radio for a pair of bridles, a slightly worn harness and a chestnut colt.

Apparently he'd heard enough.

LA FESTA DEGLI INNAMORATI
(VALENTINE'S DAY)

In the playground Niccolò and Giovanna, a girl with lovely bangs, fell deeply in love, held hands and spun in circles.

This is what Niccolò saw: earth and sky, earth and sky. He felt his heart fly out into all the world and comprehend all there was or would be.

So long as he spun, he owned the wind.

Then Giovanna let go, and Niccolò tumbled, and the earth gathered him into her arms and made him small again.

After which he fell out of love with Giovanna and almost never spoke to her again.

THE BUTCHER'S WIFE

Jacopo Scarpacci, the butcher, was a man made of meat. Broad-chested, ham-fisted, renowned for his love of mutton and beer, he bestrode his *macelleria* on Piazza Piccola like a braggadocio colossus, half bully, half clown. His manners were crude, his temper legendary; his nightly visits to the *caffè* too often ended in drunken arguments and farcical brawls.

Despite this and despite a notoriously heavy finger on the scales, Scarpacci was a master butcher, a valuable thing in a small town. He worked hard, took pride in his labors and was in turn amply rewarded. And when at the age of almost forty Jacopo decided to take a wife, he went about it with the zeal and efficiency of a man who had spent his life among livestock. On Monday he closed his shop and drove away. A week later, when he returned, he brought with him a wife.

What a wife!

Rumor had it she was a milkman's daughter from Orvieto, acquired by Scarpacci in exchange for two veal calves and a prize heifer. One glance explained this extraordinary sum. The girl was beautiful: luxuriant hair, doe-like eyes, achingly full breasts and hips, and a complexion befitting a milkman's daughter. Most of all, she was young – fully twenty years younger than the man who had purchased her hand, if not her heart. For though it was clear that Jacopo Scarpacci had fallen in love at first sight, it was not so for the girl who at sixteen had pledged her heart to a boy from a neighboring farm whose blond and sculptured physique stood in stark contrast to that of the swarthy suitor who appeared one day in her father's kitchen, reeking of offal and talking of marriage. Perhaps it was for this reason that two nights before the hastily scheduled wedding the girl, whose name was Fabrizia, ran off with her young swain, only to be plucked by her father from an outgoing train at the last minute, the swain roughly dealt with, and she returned to her home. Undeterred, the following evening she ran off again, this time to be found at dawn crouched in a neighbor's silo, threatening to do herself in.

In spite of these somewhat trivial acts of youthful rebellion, however, neither Scarpacci nor Fabrizia's father was discouraged; a deal was a deal, the terms were good, and the girl, though initially reluctant, was surely bound in the long run to honor her father's word.

So, after a wedding made notable by the groom's consumption of ale and the bride's fountain of tears, Jacopo Scarpacci returned that day to Piazza San Caterina Piccola to show off his *inamorata*, fondling her hips, patting her bottom, enjoying the envious glances of other men, among whom it was widely agreed that the blockhead of a butcher had done very well.

Though perhaps the women, had they been consulted, would have said otherwise.

That evening in preparation for his wedding night Scarpacci took a bath and, having scented himself with cologne and donned a fresh nightshirt, climbed the stairs to the bedroom to join his bride in the pleasures of matrimonial bliss.

To his surprise, he found the door locked.

After some minutes of cajoling, threatening and pleading, the new husband, his union no closer to consummation, put his foot to the door and kicked it down, only to find himself confronted with a scowl and a carving knife.

"*Vattene!*" said the object of all his desires. "Go away!"

Undaunted, Scarpacci stepped forward only to discover the bride's skills with the knife somewhat greater than expected. When the first swipe removed the buttons from his nightshirt, he felt the need to explain.

"I am the husband." he bellowed. "You are the wife. Obey!"

A second swipe of the knife sent the nightshirt to his knees.

"One step closer," explained his one-and-only, "I will split you open gizzard to gut and turn you into a steer."

Jacopo weighed his options. Perhaps, he reasoned, the girl needed more time. It was true they had only recently been introduced.

"I'll be back in an hour," he offered, determined to get off on the right foot.

"*Quando l'inferno gelerà.*" she countered. "When hell freezes over."

So it was that on the night of his wedding Jacopo Scarpacci made his bed on a cot in the barn, while the apple of his eye slept with a knife beneath her pillow.

NATURALLY a man of Jacopo Scarpacci's reputation was reluctant to breathe a word of this to his fellow townsmen. Appearances, to a man who sells meat, mean everything.

"She won't leave me alone," he bragged late at night at the *caffè*. "We couple like rabbits!"

"Then why aren't you at home?" asked Bruno Fabbro, whose days of coupling like rabbits with his wife had long faded from memory.

"Ecco. A man needs sustenance," Scarpacci boasted, downing another ale.

"He'd best watch out a fox doesn't sneak into the hutch while the buck's not watching," whispered Panzarino the Anarchist, loud enough for Scarpacci, who had ears like a rabbit, to hear, which led to the usual round of fisticuffs and broken platters.

In his more sober moments, however, Jacopo, though not by nature given to deep reflection, pondered his plight with a lover's ardent concern. Perhaps he had been too gruff; perhaps a tone of gentle kindness would unlock his tender bride's heart, among other things. With that in mind for the next few days he proved a model of attentiveness, showering his beloved with thoughtful kindnesses and lavish praise.

She ignored them.

He brought her flowers.

She chopped them to pieces.

He bought her gifts.

She threw them away.

In desperation, he went to the priest for advice.

"Two veal calves and a heifer?" said Don Federico, and whistled softly in the privacy of the confessional. "This must be quite a wife."

"She won't obey," bleated Scarpacci.

"Get her pregnant," Don Fillipo suggested. "That often seems to work."

To which Jacopo gave no reply. Given the knife beneath the bride's pillow, pregnancy was also out of the question.

"Failing that," continued Don Federico, "Prayer is all the Lord provides when it comes to women. Prayer and patience. Say one hundred fifty Our Fathers and hope for the best."

A powerful man rendered helpless by the arrows of love, Scarpacci returned to his barn with nothing more than patience and prayer to leaven his loneliness. Prayer, however, is seldom a match for frustration, which shortly begets distrust. Seeds of suspicion began to sprout in Scarpacci's heart. Perhaps Fabbro had been right; perhaps there was a fox lurking outside the hutch, the young man to whom she'd pledged herself, hidden in the shadows; or someone else, among the many men coveting her as she stood all day in the doorway of the shop, a far off look in her eye, as if waiting for some noble Galahad to come to her rescue and render Scarpacci a cuckold.

Then occurred a puzzling incident involving several small boys lurking on the fire-escape outside his window as Scarpacci took his weekly bath. While no actual harm was done, the matter became the source of merriment in the *caffè* and in Biggio's barbershop, the upshot being that Scarpacci had nearly been cuckolded by a band of cherubs.

It was all he could take. The next week he put Fabrizia in his truck and drove away.

A day later they were back.

"Don't complain to me," the bride's father had smirked as he sat milking the dairy cow Scarpacci had supplied as part of the wedding dowry. "That girl is impossible. Willful. Pig-headed. I had to deal with her for sixteen years. Why on earth would I want her back?"

When Scarpacci appealed to his sense of fairness the dairyman scoffed. "Fairness," he said, "is made of air. This cow is made of milk." In desperation, Scarpacci proffered a bribe: a lifetime supply of mutton and ham, delivered every month. The dairyman scoffed. "You made a bargain. Now live with it," were his words as he slammed the barn doors shut.

Thus bound to each other by contract and law, if not by the bonds of love, Jacopo and Fabrizia returned to his shop on Piazza Piccola where, having no other choice, they settled into domestic life, she in her bed up the stairs, he on his cot in the barn. Thwarted in his attempts at love, Jacopo immersed himself in the business he knew, that of slaughter, while Fabrizia resumed her post in the butcher shop doorway, awaiting a rescue which, as time went by, seemed less and less likely. Evenings, having locked her inside the shop, Jacopo would repair to the *caffè* to drown his regrets in tankards of beer and fisticuffs. No longer did he brag about his beautiful wife; instead, like a man saddled with bad investments, he drank to forget.

Then each night, when he arrived home, they fought.

What fights! Even to a population long used to the clarion trumpets of marital discord, the Scarpaccis' nightly battles inspired awe. From midnight to dawn the piazza echoed with their threats and recriminations. Scarpacci bellowed, Fabrizia howled. He roared; she spat. Dishes clattered and smashed. Surely, people agreed, this couldn't go on.

But things got worse. A loose board on the cellar stairs. A frayed electrical wire in the pantry. A scorpion in the bathtub, a black snake in the yard. Perhaps these were coincidence; perhaps a relationship so toxic was bound to generate insects and adders all on its own. It was as if, lacking love, the marriage was fueled by spite and hostility. Where other couples held hands, the Scarpaccis threw pots. In place of a kiss, the back of a hand. Like heavyweight boxers in a fight with no bell, it was case of last man standing. Sooner or later, all agreed, one of them would fall, by dint of sabotage, foul play, or simple exhaustion.

As it happened, it was none of those. Neither murder nor malice, but the horn of an angry *podolica* bull.

THE BULL'S HORN plunged deep into Jacopo's abdomen, turned with a twist and exited, leaving behind a gaping wound. By the time Scarpacci's stockmen had carried him across the yard and up the stairs the doctor had arrived at the scene. The doctor, whose name was Pipitone, examined Jacopo's wound, listened to his heart, then folded his stethoscope and turned to Fabrizia, who stood in the bedroom doorway, looking on, smoking a cigarette.

"Call the priest," he said, "There is nothing I can do." He closed his bag and left, leaving Fabrizia alone in the doorway while Jacopo turned from pale to ashen to deathly gray. After a while his eyes opened, and met hers.

"I have not been much of a husband," he rasped. "And you have not been much of a wife. Still, I suppose we did what we could. Now I release you. *Fa' quello che ti pare*. Do what you will."

Again, his eyes closed.

For some minutes more Fabrizia stood in the doorway as Jacopo's breathing became shallower. Perhaps she was thinking of the mess he was making of the bed. Perhaps she was thinking of the young swain in her past, to whom she had pledged her soul, but who, she had come to realize, would never appear to claim her.

Or perhaps she remembered the day a stranger – reeking of barnyard and slaughterhouse, covered with hair – stood in her father's kitchen, eyes alight with love, and asked for her hand as if she, no more than a willful milkmaid, were all the treasures of the world and more, wrapped into one.

A moment longer she stood. Then, she put out her cigarette and, stepping into the room, shut the door behind her. When, minutes later, Monsignore Federico climbed the steps, carrying with him a bag of sacramentals with which to anoint Scarpacci's soul for heaven, he found the door locked. Somewhat taken aback, he knocked.

"*Sono I,*" he called, "Don Federico."

"*Vattene!*" came a woman's reply. "Go away!"

After some minutes more of knocking, the priest, his mission no closer to consummation, put his foot to the door and kicked it open, only to find himself confronted with two bodies in bed; one deathly pale, the other a startlingly healthy pink.

"I said, get out," said Fabrizia, the pink one.

"I am the priest," replied the priest. "Obey!"

Fabrizia threw back the blanket, revealing her exquisite and utter nakedness.

"*Quando l'inferno gelerà,*" she countered.

Clutching his sacraments, the Monsignore fled.

What transpired in the minutes and hours that followed, out of sight of the dubious world; what alchemy of touch and caress, tenderness and desire, grit and determination can, without witnesses, be only surmised. How it was that a dairyman's daughter managed, without benefit of surgery – other than the crude stitches she herself administered – to heal so severe a wound, seemed to some miraculous, though to others it smacked of witchcraft. Still others, who understood the true nature of love and a lover's wounds, could only shake their heads in wonder that such an improbable thing could occur in a place as unlikely as a butcher shop on a small square in a meaningless town in the middle of nowhere.

Though perhaps only in such a place could such a thing happen.

Scarpacci the butcher did not die of his wounds that night, nor the next. When after a week the doctor was once again summoned he predicted the full recovery of the very same man he had left for dead days earlier. Even more surprisingly the following morning, to everyone's shock, the *macelleria* stood open for business. Behind the counter, in apron and cap, wielding a cleaver, trimming the fat, balancing the scales, stood the butcher's wife – who was known to be deft with the knife. By the end of the week, with the help of Scarpacci's stockmen, Fabrizia had taken up the chores of slaughtering and was reported to be a quick study. In a very short time, while her husband continued his long recuperation, her skills as a butcher came to rival even his.

Meanwhile, late at night, the resounding arguments of the past gave way to whispers of delight, as Fabrizia granted to Jacopo the tenderness he had so long desired. In return for her ministrations he produced an outpouring of gratitude which became, within weeks, a swelling in her.

Can such a thing happen? Can it be that from such rack and ruin might come such a sweet peace? Perhaps this outcome was too good to be true. Perhaps, in years to come, Jacopo and Fabrizia grew bored with their bliss, and once again fought like dogs. Then again, it is possible, though unlikely, that Fabrizia grew fat and ungainly, bearing children like apples from a tree, and when the boy from her youth arrived at last to claim her, he took one look and quietly slipped away.

It is almost certainly not true that, some years later, war having arrived, a particular *Gruppenführer* and his staff were invited to dine at loyal Scarpacci's table, only later to discover the meal they'd eaten consisted of the butcher himself, chopped and minced, along with a generous serving of arsenic and rat poison; after which the butcher's wife was not seen again until the war's end, when Fabrizia Scarpacci emerged at the forefront of haut cuisine in the booming postwar Swiss culinary industry.

In the absence of proof, however, any of these things might have occurred. After half a decade of war, as with everything else on Piazza Piccola, only possibilities remained. So one guess is as good as another.

Ognuno scelga il suo veleno.

Choose your poison.

IL PROFESSORE

At precisely one o'clock each afternoon, in the study of his apartment on Via San Marco, the young Professor is roused from his reveries by the chiming of his pocket watch. It is indisputably the timepiece of a learned scholar. Around the dial of bold Roman numerals circle the orbits of miniature planets, the stars and the sun – a map of the great universe – as well as the moon in its phases, not to mention the passage of Sirius; all moving according to principles and laws not often discussed among the earthy denizens of Piazza Santa Caterina Piccola.

Punctual as always, the professor - a tall, erect figure with a shock of unruly hair and the piercing eyes of a rational man - rises from his chair and makes his way past shelves stacked with books and journals, walls covered with honors and degrees, and a large desk arranged with photographs and letters from colleagues: Einstein, the Curies, de Beauvoir and Sartre. Donning his coat he nods to his housekeeper – though on occasion he fails to recognize her at all – puts on his hat, descends the stairs and steps out.

Hands in pockets he moves across the piazza, a figure well-known and well-liked by those who greet him, even though few of them understand the exact nature of his accomplishments in the fields of science, physics and mathematics. Fewer still – if any – have read the treatises which catapulted him to fame as a young genius of the first order, a shining intellectual light of the modern century. Nevertheless, they welcome him with smiles and tips of the hat. *"Buongiorno, Professore! Come sta oggi?"* To which the Professor simply nods and continues on his way past the shops, past the stone-sweeper Fausto who, with great ceremony, snaps to attention with his broom and salutes.

At Menucci's Caffè, with its checkered awning, he turns in.

As always at lunch hour the restaurant is crowded, waiters jostling between tables amid aromas of pasta and garlic and wine while Menucci himself barks orders. As the Professor enters, one or two patrons look up in recognition, then nudge their fellow diners, recounting in low voices the remarkable story: how, in his early thirties, overwhelmed by the demands of his own success, the young genius chose to retreat to a place where, undisturbed, he might live among his books and concentrate on theories too fragile to be subject to the whims of politics and academia. How, remarkably, Piazza Santa Caterina Piccola was the place he chose to settle.

Then, a year later, the accident.

"*Professore!*" booms Menucci over the noise. "On time, as usual!" With a knowing wink to the others, he gestures grandly toward the kitchen doors.

"At your pleasure, *egregio!*"

Stepping into the kitchen the scholar makes his way past the chef, who is at the moment berating the busboys; through a maze of culinary staff, all of whom are used to his presence here. Finding his place, he hangs his coat and hat on hooks on the storeroom door – first the coat, then the hat – lifts an apron from a pile of fresh linens and, tying it on, turns to the sink.

The water, he observes, is properly hot, already frothy with soap. *Perfetto.*

He reaches for a plate and, whistling quietly, happily sets to work at his job washing dishes.

LOOKING BACK, the vectors were calculable, especially for a mind such as his: angle of descent, rate of acceleration, effects of friction. A man crossing the street, a runaway bricklayer's cart descending the hill. The variables: a moment's delay, a step in either direction, the merest gust of wind. The vectors collide; the equation collapses. Thrown through the air, cranium impacts stone.

What a jumble! Phyla and genera, differential equations, Avogadro's number, Riemann's hypothesis, the location of Kiribati, the structures of numbers and crystals and molecules, knocked loose all at once from their well-ordered shelves. The merging of north-west-south, the disappearance of names, the failure of language; the shape of the pyramids, scrambled, tossed, like Alice in Wonderland, into the swirling void. Into that crater tumbled Euripides, Alpha and Sigma, Kant and Kierkegaard; poetry and recipes; a trip to the lake when he was six; a furry dog; his name; his mother's kiss.

In that moment, as the bricklayer's cart continued down the hill, was there some final, magnificent revelation? Did all knowledge merge into one single, unified whole?

⌒‿

THE WATER SWIRLS in a vortex as he pulls the last plate out, glinting with pearls of light from overhead. Around the perimeter of the plate a caravan of bubbles – globular, perfect – cling to the curve, flowing sideways, not downward. *The plate is round; it has no beginning. The light moves fast; how fast? The water swirls. The plate is round; it has no beginning....*

From the pocket of his coat on the hook comes the chime of his watch. Nine PM. He turns from the sink, removes his apron, reaches for his hat and coat. On his way home he might see the moon.

What is the moon?

Later in his rooms, surrounded by books he cannot read, letters he cannot answer, given shelter by people of whom he has no knowledge or memory, the Professor eats the dinner the housekeeper has provided and recalls, with some detail, the water on the plate. Sideways it flowed, not down.

Sideways, not down.

It stays in his mind. Will it happen again tomorrow?

He smiles. Tomorrow, he will see.

LA BEFANA

Eight days before Christmas, the good Christians of Piazza Santa Caterina Piccola – farmers and merchants, thieves and apostles, neighbors and nemeses – squeezed together into the pews of San Bartolomeo Giusto. Amid the sound of bells and the smell of incense and cow manure, Monsignore Don Federico intoned the prayers of the Novena. From the back pew the fool Fausto howled his fervent responses. Mamma and Niccolo attended. Nonno stayed home, having reached an age where he knew better.

After Mass, Mamma and Niccolò lit candles in honor of Mamma's family and for Papà who was far away. Mamma said each candle was a special prayer, one that God Himself would answer. When her eyes were closed Niccolò lit a candle and prayed for the safe recovery of his broken statue, half of which lay entombed beneath the storm drain in the piazza. Perhaps, Niccolò suggested, God might intercede; even speak to La Befana, the wandering gift-giver who brought presents to all good children on Epiphany Eve.

"Niccolò!" hissed Mamma, looking over. "Don't shut your eyes so tight! Your head will burst!"

"*Sì, Mamma*," said Niccolò. His prayer, he knew, was futile: La Befana brought gifts to good children only. For the others – the bad ones – she left onions and coal.

The fact was, with her ragged broomstick and searching eyes, La Befana frightened Niccolò. Each year he made sure to sleep with Mamma until the specter had come and gone, although this year he'd made up his mind he wouldn't.

Despite these concerns, for Niccolò the days before *Natale* were filled with music and light, most of all with good things to eat. The bakery shelves burst with honeyed *struffoli* and sugary *cenci* and marzipan fruits and *pandoro*. At school Maestra Leonora had the children dress in sandals and shepherds' hats and go from classroom to classroom playing songs on shepherds' pipes. One afternoon at the *farmacia*, beneath the very nose of Boldoni the nearsighted pharmacist, Niccolò and his friends filled their pockets with candy, then hid in Rinaldo's outhouse and feasted til Quindici got sick.

One night it snowed, and they made angels in the drifts beneath the statue of Garibaldi.

Most exciting of all, the arrival of the season had brought the sounds of saws and hammers to the square, where a team of men led by Abele Bassevi, the carpenter, began work on the platform to hold the *Presepio*, the annual Nativity scene. The whole town pitched in, hauling lumber, fitting joists, delivering bales of hay. Nonno climbed high on the rafters to hang strings of colored lights. Niccolò was allowed to hold the nails. Fausto, who considered himself in charge of all things on the Piazza, took a proprietary role, hounding the workmen, barking orders and waving his arms.

When the manger was complete it was time to retrieve from Abele Bassevi's workshop the figures of the Holy Family, carved in wood by Bassevi's grandfather decades ago. The workshop, up the hill from the bakery and overlooking the distant mountains, had been occupied by Abele's family for as long as anyone knew, perhaps for centuries. Large oaken doors opened into a cavernous studio populated by snarling saws, rattling lathes and workbenches laden with axes, chisels, braces and files. Here, amidst piles of sawdust and the reek of carpenter's glue, Abele and his assistant performed their craftsmen's alchemy, transforming humble boards into graceful, swan-like forms: cabinets and bedsteads, tables and chairs.

But to Niccolò the true magic waited in the darkness of the storage bins in the far corner of the studio. Looming in the shadows, silent, abiding, stood great wooden figures, larger than life: the Holy Family, awaiting their annual summons to the Piazza. Joseph the father, his brow furrowed with burden; the Magi and shepherds, wide-eyed and believing; the donkey, the camel, the winged angels; most of all Mary, beautiful and serene, whose breasts through her flowing robes as she knelt before the young Savior's crib caused a curious itch in Niccolò's loins. Finally, nestled in the curving, ark-like safety of his crib lay the infant Jesus, swaddled against the cold of the Bethlehem night, a fine layer of sawdust perched on the curve of His tiny halo.

One by one the massive figures were lifted from their bins by Abele and his men and carried into the sudden light of day to be roped into place on the wagon. Then it was down the hill toward the square, cart wheels rattling on cobblestone, the wooden figures, bound and jostling, struggling to maintain their dignity while a crowd of schoolchildren, who had been given the afternoon off from school, shouted and pranced alongside like wild pagans. To some the scene, with its raucous crowd and tumbrel full of stoic prisoners, seemed reminiscent of certain long-ago public executions, though surely such barbarism had long ago come and gone.

Having reached the Piazza the figures – all but the Infant Jesus Himself, who would not be delivered until Christmas Eve – were set into position in the manger, accompanied by the usual arguments over which piece went where as well as whispered jokes concerning the camel and sheep. All the while Fausto, pretending to be a Wise Man himself, strutted across the stage and, egged on by the men, showered blessings on the crowd.

"Wise man, my ass!" shouted Fabbro, the stablemaster.

"Keep him away from the camel!" yelled De Campo the mason. Laughter rose all around as Fausto mugged.

"Yid!" called a voice next to Niccolò and the laughter continued anyway, as if no one had heard, or cared to hear, though Nonno on the stage turned to look.

The man who had shouted turned to the group he was with and said loudly, for everyone to hear, "The woodcarver's a Jew. What business does he have in our holiday?" He pointed to the platform. "Jew statues. Maybe someone should look in crib, eh? *Gesù con il cazzone di un ebreo.*" At the mention of which – the Holy Child with the prick of a Jew – the other young men in black shirts snickered. One or two spat on the cobblestones. On the platform Nonno set down his hammer, but the young men were already moving off, among them Vincenzo Nutti, walking at the edge of the group as if unsure of his standing.

On the platform Abele Bassevi appeared not to have taken notice, so it was hard to tell if he had heard. When the blackshirts were gone the laughter and good-natured joking resumed, and Fausto pretended to fall in love with the camel, and the incident was forgotten, or nearly so.

Then evening came and Nonno connected the wires to the colored lights. The square lit up in miraculous hues, and the wooden statues came alive with a heavenly glow, their days of exile triumphantly redeemed. Monsignore Federico arrived to bless the scene and Signora Michelli the manicurist, who had once sung at La Scala (or so she said), knelt at the platform and trilled "Ave Maria" while the sky turned from deep purple to black.

Later that night in the rooms above the bakery Nonno lighted the Yule log – the *Ceppo* – and Niccolò stared into the fire for hours. In the fire he saw many things: sometimes a lion, or a battle scene, armies fighting and towers falling in the flames; then Papà, walking the streets of New York, alone in the great and mysterious city.

"Niccolò!" said Mamma. "What are you thinking about?"

"Niente," said Niccolò.

Mamma laughed. "All that staring for nothing? My poor little empty-headed boy!" And she hugged him and put him to bed.

"Will Papà have Christmas?" he asked.

"Everyone has Christmas," said Mamma. She kissed him and pulled up his sheet.

By now, Niccolò was very sleepy. "Mamma," he said. *"Il cazzone di Gesù.* Is it like mine, or a Jew's?"

Mamma took him to the sink and washed his mouth out with soap.

Christmas Eve was a day of fasting. All morning Rinaldo and Quindici loitered in the piazza while their mothers began to prepare the *cenone*, the Christmas meal, to be served the next day. Until then there would be nothing to eat but fish soup. Nonno offered Niccolò a pinch of tobacco to quell his appetite but Niccolò, suspecting a trap, refused.

In the afternoon Nonno and Bassevi delivered the Infant Jesus to the manger. Niccolò rode in the cart. When no one was looking he snuck a glance at the Baby's *cazzone*.

Folded in its skin, it was hard to tell if it was *ebreo* or not.

By dark the weather had turned windy and cold. Outside, beneath the glare of the electric lights on the platform, the Holy Family huddled, isolated and exposed, at the mercy of innkeepers and unchristian Kings; while in the bakery it was warm, and smelled of marzipan and anisette and succulent meats and the perfume of candles as Nonno, by the stove, recited to Niccolò and Mamma the old and compelling legends of many years past.

And it seemed to Niccolò that God's Presence grew close and pressed inward upon them, the ineffable proof of His Goodness, His gifts and His unending mercies, hovering over each household, over each mother and child.

Then came shouts from the square, a flickering of light on the walls, and everyone ran to see the *Presepio* in flames.

THE FIRE ROARED UP from the hay bales, paused briefly to gauge its own strength, then sprang across the platform onto the backs of the camel and sheep, which trembled, then burst into light, the camel drooping slowly to its knees, the sheep stock-still, as if transfixed by a brilliant dawn.

Relentless, the flames reached the walls of the manger and engulfed the shepherds, climbing their staffs to ignite the angels' wings, then the poor angels themselves, who might have flown, but stayed to protect their Lord.

In the gathering crowd there were shouts for water; men were already approaching with buckets. As Niccolò and Mamma raced across the square the Piazza glowed with a hideous light. The fire overtook the Wise Men and crept toward the cradle where Joseph and Mary, intent on their adorations, knelt in worship, oblivious to all else. Then they too were blazing pyres, dark smoke billowing into heaven as overhead the strings of lights came loose and descended, bulbs still flickering.

Impossibly, in the roaring fire was a man: alive, ablaze, dancing among the flames.

"Ahhhhh!" cried the crowd in astonishment.

The figure – shepherd or magus, seemingly brought to life by the fire – lurched from the back of the stable, hair and clothes alight, arms flailing, spinning like a dervish toward the burning cradle. A board underneath gave way.

"Ohhhhhh," moaned the spectators.

The thing staggered forward, lifted the baby Jesus from His cradle then, infant in arms, staggered ahead and collapsed at the edge of the platform. Hands reached up from the crowd to pull him to safety and pluck from his head his fiery aviator's cap. Seconds later the stage collapsed in a shower of sparks, swallowing with one great, groaning gulp grandfather Bassevi's wooden family.

The fire burned all night, despite the best efforts of Municipal Engine Company #2, who left the scene at midnight having coated Piazza Piccola with a slippery and dangerous sheet of ice. In the grey fog of dawn Don Federico and Don Tommaso made their way across the now-treacherous stones to bless the wreckage, particularly the remains of the Savior Child, blistered and charred, which had been left to burn itself out in the very spot where, some days before, snow angels had been laid.

As for Fausto, *lo stolto*, who had gone to sleep in the manger and awakened half in flames, his escape with minor burns seemed miraculous, though it is probable his many layers of filthy rags and leather aviator's cap had more to do with his quick recovery than Providence.

The next afternoon it snowed again, extinguishing the last of the embers and covering the square in a merciful shroud of white. Ten days later, on the Feast of the Epiphany, the wreckage had been swept and cleared, though on the pavement could still be seen ghostly images of Bassevi's sculptures, charred into the stones, darkly foreshortened, as if reaching up from below.

DESPITE THESE EVENTS, or perhaps because of them, the Feast seemed more festive than ever. In church the revelation of God the Son as a human being was announced by Don Fillipo with more than usual flamboyance, though notably absent were the ear-shattering responses from Fausto, who had temporarily lost his voice in the fire.

After Mass Niccolò walked with his grandfather up the hill to Abele Bassevi's workshop. The gates hung open, the studio stripped, the place abandoned. Nonno made up a story that Abele had gone to live with his family in Bologna, but Niccolò saw through it. How, he reasoned, could Bassevi's family be elsewhere when they'd lived in this place for two hundred years?

Scrawled on the gates in white paint were the words *"Ebreo"* and *"Yid."*

"Che cosa?" Niccolo said to his grandfather.

Nonno shook his head and kicked some stones. "*Chi lo sa.*" he said, "Who knows?" Then they walked down the hill back to town.

That night Niccolò hung his stocking in expectation of the visit from *La Befana*, who had, on a starlit evening long ago, failed to accompany the Wise Men to Bethlehem and was therefore fated to roam the world leaving gifts for deserving *bambini* – although perhaps not for Niccolò. He had heard the stories of willful children who, late at night, felt the angry thump of *Befana's* broom on their backsides; nevertheless, true to his promise to himself, he went to sleep in his own bed.

When the hours went by and he couldn't sleep he called to Mamma, who was never far away, who came and sang to him in her gentle voice...

Viene, viene la Befana
Vien dai monti a notte fonda
Come è stanca! la circonda
Neve e gelo e tramontana!

Niccolò felt his eyes grow heavy and his fears indistinct as her voice surrounded him in this most impermanent creche, under the stars, with danger lurking all around.

She comes from the mountains in the deep of the night
Look how tired she is! All wrapped up
In snow and frost and the north wind!
Viene, viene la Befana!

THE VISITATION

It began, as always, with something trivial: in this case Mussolini's nose. "It's crooked," observed Ennio Baldelli the haberdasher, browsing the pages of *L'Unità* while waiting his turn in the chair at Luigi Biggio's barbershop, on an afternoon when the world – at least the world of Piazza Piccola – had nothing better to do.

"*Che sciocchezza*," growled Bruno Fabbro, who managed the stables across the street and was known to admire *Il Duce*. "It's a fine nose. A manly nose. A Roman nose."

"I didn't say it wasn't manly. Or Roman," replied Baldelli. "Just crooked."

"What's wrong with a crooked nose?" said Arturo Pascoli, Biggio's brother-in-law and assistant barber, whose wife, as everyone knew, possessed a nose like a scimitar. So no one replied.

There the discussion might have ended and taken its place among the countless other meaningless colloquies between human beings which daily fly out the windows of barbershops in towns the world over, to be scattered, forgotten, among the four winds. Except for a sudden thought that struck Ernesto Capelli, the night concierge at the Grand Hotel Imperiale, whose face at that moment was covered in shaving lather.

"It's all the woman's fault," said Capelli.

An observation which led to an event concerning which, from that day on, the men who were present refuse to speak or even acknowledge, perhaps even to themselves.

All this happened – if it happened at all – amid the fragrant and collegial comforts of Luigi Biggio's barbershop, three doors down from Mamma's bakery. Here, among the aromas of lotion and colognes and the clap of the razor strop, the most eminent minds of Piazza Piccola, along with Biggio's pet goat, gathered each week to resolve the great issues of Italy and the world, compete at *scopone* and chess, escape their wives and have their whiskers trimmed in the two barber chairs manned by Luigi and Arturo. In the *negozio di barberia* almost anything might be discussed, though when it came to delicate subjects Biggio's young nephew Gustavo, who swept the floors, would be asked to set down his broom and wait outside until things had been resolved. And though disagreements were not unusual, unlike the *caffè* across the square where an abundance of wine tended to lead to nightly brawls, in Biggio's barbershop things were more civilized, partly because Biggio himself held the razor, partly because a plaster bust of the Madonna kept watch from a niche above the shelves of shaving cups and toilet water, gazing down in tolerant, if slightly vexed, benediction at the proceedings below.

In any event...

"What woman?" said Biggio, razor in hand, as he stepped back to size up Capelli's mustache.

"The one who fired the shot that went through *il Duce's* nose," replied Capelli.

Indeed, this event had actually occurred some years previously, the female assassin imprisoned for life and Mussolini, the sturdy "Iron Prefect," long recovered.

"*Una pazza*," grunted Fabbro, taking a seat in Arturo's chair. "Crazy out of her mind."

"They're all out of their minds," suggested Arturo. "*Tutti.*"

From around the shop came nods of assent, for on the subject of women and madness there was seldom disagreement among married men.

"My wife." said Baldelli, "Talks to ladybugs."

"My wife makes the bed upside down on Mondays," confessed Biggio.

"My wife," admitted Fabbro, "burns my toenail clippings for luck."

"It's the same the world over," said Baldelli, "It's been true ever since *Adamo ed Eva.*"

At the mention of Adam, the nods became solemn, as if in memory of a brother-in-arms, cut down in the bloom of youth by a cruel and undeserved fate.

"At least Adam's wife was beautiful" mused Capelli. "That's why he ate the apple."

"Temptation," said Baldelli. "What man is immune to its bite? Only a priest or a saint!"

The boy, Gustavo, paused in his sweeping to cross himself. Biggio's goat looked out the window and yawned.

"The fact is," said Fabbro. "I'm often tempted. Who wouldn't be, with a wife like mine? Always nagging, complaining. 'Bruno do this! Bruno do that!' There isn't a day I don't wish myself a free man."

"And then what would you do?" asked Baldelli, dubiously.

"Find a beautiful woman who appreciated a man of my type," said Fabbro.

From around the shop came hoots of derision. "What type is that, Fabbro?" asked Ignacci.

"A man of the stables," mocked Baldelli. "'Ooh Bruno, *caro mio*, I love the smell of horse manure. Kiss me again!'"

"Laugh all you like," growled Fabbro, "But don't tell me you haven't thought the same."

"Trust me," said Biggio, "The woman you're looking for doesn't exist. At least, not around here."

"What about next door, at the bakery?" said Capelli, "There's a beautiful woman."

"*È sposata*. She's married," pointed out Biggio.

"*Sposata, non sposata*, maybe so, maybe not" Fabbro shrugged. "Her husband goes away, what, almost a year now?"

"Married <u>and</u> faithful," said Biggio, who greatly admired the baker's wife, who, it seemed to him, always reserved for him her brightest smile as she handed him his packages across the counter; although if he were to admit, in her eyes one could read a note of wistfulness, as if regretting a path not taken. A young girl, he thought, barely a women herself, was too young to wear such a look of worry.

"*Ecco!* You see?" said Fabbro, rousing Biggio from his reverie. "What harm is there? A man dreams. What else can we do?"

"Speaking of temptation…" said Baldelli, nodding his head toward the front window. Everyone followed his gaze, including the goat. Across the square stood Scarpacci's butcher shop, in the doorway of which, at that very moment, stood a raven-haired woman smoking a cigarette, eyes upturned to the sky, while a group of small boys near the statue of Garibaldi whispered and pointed.

"*Ragazzi…*" whispered Fabbro.

"*Che donna…*" said Badelli, shaking his head.

"*Mamma mia…*" sighed the boy, Gustavo.

"Gustavo!" bellowed Biggio. "Wait outside."

Gustavo set down his broom and went out the door, passing Riccardo Ignacci, the hotel maître d', on his way in.

"What have I missed?" said Ignacci, as the shop bell above him tinkled and rang.

"Scarpacci's wife," nodded Fabbro.

"*Adamo ed Eva,*" corrected Arturo.

"Mussolini's nose," said Ennio Baldelli.

"Ah," said Ignacci, instantly understanding all. "Women. We are ever in their thrall, are we not?"

"Slaves," nodded Baldelli.

"Beasts of burden," added Fabbro.

Not one of them noticed as, from above, an almost imperceptible shower of dust drifted down among them as, perhaps moved by the breeze from the doorway, the plaster Madonna shifted in her niche.

SO IT WENT for another half hour among this exalted council while Biggio's goat lay basking in sunlight; while outside in the square the horseflies buzzed around Morelli's vegetable cart; while the flags atop the Grand Hotel Imperiale sagged in the indolent afternoon heat; while a gang of small boys conceived a plan to spy on the butcher's wife; while the wheels of history ground silently toward the distant thunder of war. Inside the *barberia* a list of grievances took shape, seeds of long-withheld discontent suddenly bursting forth. Several times was Gustavo banished, then readmitted, only to be banished again as the list of crimes and outrages grew ever longer.

"Look what we put up with," said Capelli as Biggio applied hot towels to Baldelli's face. "No matter what we do, it's never enough."

"I work my hands to the bone," groused Fabbro "Just to put food on her plate, what thanks do I get? I work harder, she gets fatter. *Non la si spunta mica* – you can't win."

"My wife says I'm lazy," groused Ignacci, who was known to be the laziest man on Piazza Piccola, so once again no one replied. Instead Luigi Biggio, perhaps regretting his daydream concerning the baker's wife and her wistful eyes, attempted to stem the tide.

"Nevertheless," he announced. "We are men who cherish our wives, and owe them gratitude for the many graces they provide us."

"Graces?!" snorted Fabbro. "Broken backs, more likely!"

"They'll ride us like mules to our graves!" muttered Baldelli.

"Why do we endure this?" scowled Capelli. "Why do we, who shoulder the burdens, who wear the pants, allow such injustice?"

"Someone should do something," whined Arturo.

Fabbro rose from Arturo's chair and – catching a glimpse of himself in the mirror, freshly dusted with talcum and reeking of *eau de toilette* and liking very much what he saw – addressed the gathering with the *éclat* of Garibaldi at the gates of Naples.

"Hear what I say!" he roared. "No more should we bind ourselves in chains to this tyranny of women. No more should we cower in fear! No more submit!"

Incredibly, at least to Gustavo, Fabbro's cry was taken up.

"We must teach them," bellowed Capelli, "The man's word is law!

"The man is the boss!" Arturo shouted. *"È l'uomo che comanda!"*

And for that small moment in that small place there burned in the hearts of men an engendered fire, an ancient brotherhood, a primal memory of a long-lost dominion.

Then, a noise.

High over their heads, something skittered and stirred. Biggio, reaching for vial of *Acqua di Selva*, looked up in alarm as, in the niche directly above, like the figurehead of a great ship, the leading edge of his plaster Madonna loomed into view. Indomitable, undeterred, she topped the shelf, teetered, and plunged downward with the fury of an avenging angel, smashing through mirrored shelves, shattering glass and launching vials in all directions, which in turn exploded into fragments upon impact with the marble floor, sending shards of pottery through the rising dust as all around, the conspirators scurried for cover. One fragment nearly severed the tip of Baldelli's nose; another spun into the rear of Biggio's sleeping goat who, suddenly awakened, emitted a bleat of pain and panicked, leaping through Biggio's window and into the square with a crash loud enough to alarm Morelli's horse, who bolted in fear and fled, dumping a wagonload of vegetables across the piazza.

In the moments that followed, as the plaster began to settle, there loomed a profound silence. Biggio reached into the rubble to hand Baldelli a towel for his nose. Gustavo began sweeping.

No words were exchanged.

None were required.

AS TO EXPLANATIONS for the events at Biggio's *barberia* that afternoon – justifications, revelations, – there were none, at least not from those who were actually there. Others who were not suggested earthquakes as the cause, though no one had felt the slightest tremor. Still others blamed Biggio's goat. Among the men who had witnessed the occurrence, however, an *omertà* was put in place. Never again was it be mentioned, especially amongst themselves.

That night Baldelli returned home with flowers; Capelli with perfume; Biggio with wine; Ignacci and Arturo with all three. Each made sure to do the cooking; all made love to their wives.

And that Sunday, as well as several Sundays following, they all went to Mass.

Just in case.

THE WOMAN IN THE
CAFFÉ

D own the narrow mountain road that led from Monte Castella, across a wide river half a thousand miles toward the sea, one came to a place as unlike Piazza Santa Caterina Piccolo as the wolf to the newborn lamb: a great City, streamlined and modern, center of light and culture, art and ideas, gleaming motorcars and elegant nightclubs. Here men who had hooked their fortunes to a New Order conspired to shape the destinies of millions while around them, like chimeric manifestations of their own self-importance, hovered women of uncanny beauty and poise, floating like feathers on the breezes of fashion and chic.

Gianna Massimi was one such feather.

Where she came from was no one's concern; in this place a woman's past was irrelevant. Her looks were her currency, and Gianna's were priceless. Slender as a reed, curved like a lily, wrapped in the furs of her latest admirers, her clever eyes and elegant lips approached perfection. But though her beauty was transcendent, her soul was transparent. At twenty-two she'd already had many *liaisons*, each for a short while only, and none whose attentions had left the slightest mark on her heart.

There was a reason for this. She had no heart to be marked.

It wasn't that she was jaded, or blasé. She simply felt no emotions: not pity or envy, jealousy or spite, not sorrow nor joy and most certainly not love. Pinch her and she jumped, tickle her and she giggled, but in matters of the heart she was numb. Not that this had proved a disadvantage in her career; quite the opposite, her aura made her irresistible to men, for what her lovers mistook for passion in her eyes was simply the reflection of their own ardor, their own feverish lust and fervent hopes. One after another they attempted to conquer the Everest of her heart; one after another they failed. In a world obsessed by appearances Gianna glittered like a diamond, but her essence was stone.

Naturally she told no one of her condition; to admit such a thing would invite the jackals. She was, however, mildly curious about it. She studied the women around her, swooning from passion, bathing in heartbreak. She scanned the Sonnets for clues; she read the story of Pinocchio, the wooden boy who ached to be human. Occasionally in a haze of champagne and cocaine or a handsome suitor's embrace she imagined some *frisson* of emotion, but each time it turned out to be a mirage. No matter; her secret, it seemed, was her success. Season after season she floated upward through endless rounds of parties, affairs and bedrooms, adored for her looks, attracting and discarding ever more powerful lovers, a young woman envied by many and desired by all. Still, despite all that, she couldn't escape, on occasion, the nagging notion that one should feel *something*.

Shouldn't one?

NOT SURPRISINGLY in this sophisticated and world-weary society there existed a thirst for diversion, the more extravagant the better. Clairvoyants and mediums were all the rage, available day and night to amuse, console or terrify their wealthy patrons. Late one evening Gianna found herself in the candlelit parlor of a popular mystic and reader of cards, Madama Vadoma, known as the One-Eyed Gypsy, whose talent for prediction was said to be infallible, not to mention attractively overpriced. This night the Madama, having attended first to a Calabrian count whose boudoir was haunted by his naked mother, then an Austrian heiress involved in a tryst with her brother's chauffeur, turned her attention to the striking young woman lounging in a corner divan, idly blowing smoke rings from her pearl-inlaid *quellazaire*.

"And you, *Signorina*," she asked. "Have you a ghost in your life?"

Gianna Massimi yawned. "Ghosts," she purred, "are a bore."

The Gypsy adjusted her bracelets. "A lost loved one, perhaps. A mysterious dream."

Gianna shrugged and glanced at her nails.

Something about her complete dispassion intrigued Madama. "A secret then. One that sets you apart from all others. Something you've shared with no one."

The faintest spark of interest in the girl's eyes told her she'd found the mark. She leaned closer, as if to pluck a clue from the depths of the young beauty's indifference.

"You have a wish. It yearns to be free. Release it, *la mia principessa*. Tell me."

In the low light the parlor lay silent as a tomb. The heiress had left; the Count dozed on the couch. The smell of incense hovered like a cloud. Gianna hesitated.

"*Voglio sentire,*" she whispered.

The candle flickered; the Gypsy's eye glittered. "*Così?*"

"I want to feel," repeated Gianna.

"Feel...what?"

"Anything. Everything. *Tutti.* Can you help me?"

For the briefest moment Madama Vadoma considered this request, then reached for her cards. Turning one over, she arched an eyebrow. "As it happens," she said, "there is a remedy for your condition. It will, however, require a journey." She pointed to the card: eight cups and a robed traveler with a cane. "You must go to a faraway place. A simple place, unsullied by duplicity and deceit. There you will find the relief you seek."

Gianna eyed the card, intrigued. "What place is that?"

Madama turned another card. "A tiny hamlet. A paradise in the mountains. There you will find your true heart."

"How?"

The Gypsy gestured for silence. Closing her eye she moaned, and became one with the spirit world, her voice rich with the infinite. "When you get there," she intoned, "you will find a well. Drink of the water. At midnight. A single cupful, no more."

"And the name of this place?"

The table trembled. The chandelier rattled. Leaning forward the one eyed gypsy whispered a name in Gianna's ear.

"Remember," she said, "But a single cupful. *Non dimenticare!*"

On the couch the Count awoke with a snort. The gas lights came on. The séance was over. The bill was paid and everyone left, well entertained. Alone in her parlor Madama Vadoma loosened her corsets, counted her fees and set about emptying ashtrays, confident that by dawn the young beauty with the pearl-handled *quellazair* would have forgotten all about the tiny and misbegotten hill town at the ends of the earth where once she'd spent a single afternoon, years ago, and vowed never to set foot in again.

THREE DAYS LATER Gianna Massimi stepped from her hired car into the dust and noise of Piazza San Caterina Piccola. Flies buzzed, donkeys brayed, goats meandered, peasants called to each other in uncouth accents. The pungent odor of manure hung in the air.

Perhaps, she thought, the Gypsy had been mistaken.

Having endured the bone-jarring journey up the winding mountain road, however, she made up her mind to stay, at least until morning. Holding her scarf to her nose she picked her way across the piazza into the lobby of the Grand Hotel Imperiale where the desk clerk, wondering what business such a creature, draped in jewelry and fur, could have in a place like his, showed her to his best available room - a musty parlor, the walls threadbare, the plumbing noisy, a far cry from her gold-trimmed apartments at the Majestic in Rome. Draping her ermine cape across a faded ottoman Gianna moved to the window and gazed down upon the piazza. What she saw did nothing to bolster her spirits: the place was a tableau of backwardness: primitive, artless and rude. Wagons clattered across the cobblestones; ragged urchins played in the dust. A goggle-eyed rustic swept stones with a battered broom. A fruit-seller stood in deep conversation with his horse. At the central well a flock of toothless washerwomen pointed and gabbled. A crude stone hut squatted next to the steps of a ponderous church.

"Paradise in the mountains," Madama Vadoma had called it. Gianna began to suspect she'd been had.

Pulling the drapes she drew a bath and ordered supper in the room, a barely edible paste of rice, corn, lard and cheese. As evening fell she painted her nails and prepared to retire, making plans to leave at dawn. With an early start she might keep a rendezvous with a wealthy munitions manufacturer on his yacht off Capri. She got into bed – a worn-out bag of lumps with sheets like sandpaper – and dozed, paying no attention to the raucous laughter of the unruly peasantry beneath her window.

At midnight, however, she woke, the words of the Gypsy in her ear.

"Drink from the water of the well at midnight. Don't forget! Non dimenticare!"

Despite her doubts, and thinking herself most definitely a fool, she rose, put on her wrap and descended to the lobby, empty but for a switchboard operator in a white fedora who turned away as she passed. Outside, the piazza lay silent in the moonlight. No headlights or streetlights, no rush of traffic, no bursts of laughter from tipsy party-goers; only the occasional bark of a dog or cry of a child. A cat crossed her path and merged into the night. She crossed, heels echoing on the cobblestones, to the central well, where a bucket hung suspended, ladle gleaming in the moonlight, almost as if expecting her. Wondering how she'd found herself in this improbable situation she dipped the ladle and drank.

The water was bitter. It tasted of mud and soil and the faint aroma of sheep. She set the ladle back in the bucket and returned to her room. Once again she undressed and made herself as comfortable as possible in the lumpy bed, pulling the rough sheets about her. She was quite sure now she'd been an imbecile to listen to a one-eyed charlatan.

Tomorrow, she told herself, she'd be done with this place.

She felt nothing.

She slept.

WAKING THE NEXT morning it struck her as peculiar that the bed, which had seemed so disagreeable the evening before, now felt oddly comforting, as if embracing her in a warm cocoon. In the soft light of dawn the room, so shabby the previous afternoon, had taken on a simple charm, sunlight streaming through her window, sparkling with dancing motes. Breakfast arrived, compliments of the hotel, a surprisingly savory mixture of Northern cuisine. As she ate she found herself for the first time in years recalling her childhood home far away in the Pyrenees: a bed not unlike this one, the smell of cooking, her mother's voice, her father's gentle laugh, and a young shepherd boy who waited for her each day at the bend in the lane. Puzzled, she rose and dressed, thinking how her friends in the city would be amused by the tale of her mistaken adventure in this improbable place.

She caught herself in the mirror, smiling.

Outside on the piazza the dust of the previous day had subsided; even the smell from the stables seemed almost pleasantly *piccante*. The square was alive with the rhythms of horses' hooves and wagon wheels and the calls of daily commerce. As Gianna crossed the piazza the muted colors of the buildings shimmered in the gentle light, composing themselves as a painting. Were she an artist, she thought, she might capture it and share it with the world.

She had always wanted to paint.

A pack of children raced past, shouting and playing, full of hope and life, their voices echoing across the square. Their joy was contagious. She recalled her own childhood friends – and again the boy at the end of the lane, the first boy she kissed. She felt her heart flutter remembering the taste of his lips and her own long-ago breathless joy. The thought made her hungry again. As if by some magic a bakery window beckoned. As she opened the door and stepped inside her nostrils filled with the heavenly aroma of fresh breads, pastries and delicious pies.

"*Che bella giornata, eh?*" A young woman, beautiful without lipstick or rouge, brushed a hair from her cheek and smiled from behind the bakery counter. In her simple smock and apron she seemed happy, and free. Nearby a wiry old man drew a Pallet of fresh-baked pastries from the oven.

"*Sì, così bello.*" Gianna ordered a warm *biscotti*. As she waited she noticed a small boy watching her from the doorway, wide-eyed at her stylish ermine and earrings.

"Niccolò! Mind your manners!" called the young woman. The boy blushed. Gianna laughed, moved by the simple tenderness between mother and child. Seeing her reflection in the glass she made up her mind to find a shop and purchase clothes more appropriate for this simple and unpretentious town.

It occurred to her it had been ages since she'd written her mother.

The biscotti arrived, filling her mouth with unexpected delight - worthy, she marveled, of the finest *pasticcerias* in the city. When she'd finished she thanked the young woman and stepped outside, humming a tune, one her mother had sung to her as a child, about a songbird in a berry bush. Church bells rang, echoing in the square. Her heart soared; she felt young again.

She forgot all about her rendezvous on Capri.

For the rest of the afternoon Gianna Massimi wandered among the streets and alleys, alive to the tapestry of life all around her. Opera music played from an open window. A baby slept in its mother's arms. Two lovers kissed beneath an awning; it made her heart spring open with yearning and envy. She went to a movie and laughed until tears streamed down her cheeks, even though she suspected it was meant to be sad. She bought a simple smock and changed in her room, then removed her lipstick and rouge.

In the mirror she looked like a girl again.

When evening fell, she joined the *passeggiata* of good people, hardworking, generous, sharing their laughter, their sense of hope and promise in this enchanted place beneath the full moon. She began to think perhaps she might stay in this gentle paradise forever; fall in love, devote herself to a simple man, grow vegetables, paint and have babies.

At midnight, still alive with excitement, she made her way once again across the cobblestones to the well. In the moonlight the ladle beckoned. Ignoring the warnings of the clairvoyant – "a single cupful, no more!" – she drank again.

The water tasted of clouds and stars and the ineffable sweetness of being. She returned to her room and went to sleep.

In the night it began to rain.

BY MORNING THE GUTTERS along Piazza Piccolo burbled and sang. Fog blanketed the distant hills. To Gianna, nestled in her sheets, it all seemed perfect.

Perhaps too perfect.

The rain on the roof stirred memories, things she'd forgotten or put out of her mind long ago. Again she recalled her home, far away: her mother's voice, her father's laugh. Now came the hint of another memory: an argument, voices raised, angry words, her defiant scorn, her mother's tears, her father's curse, her distain for their provincial ways. She'd packed a bag and left, vowing never to return. So long ago. What had become of them? And the boy in the lane?

The thought made her uneasy. She rose, dressed quickly, skipping breakfast, and went out.

On the piazza the sounds of the morning rose like a symphony in the mist: the calls of the draymen, the clop of hooves, the gentle lowing of sheep. The cool air refreshed her. She paused to breathe in the unsullied purity of this place, its quaint charm, its beautiful peasantry.

"*Stai alla larga! Stand clear!*" bellowed a voice. A wagon burst from the fog, close by, iron wheels shrieking, drawn by a dull-eyed ox. Startled, Gianna stepped back. From his seat the driver - his face weathered and old before its time, back bent from ceaseless toil, fingers missing, his coat a tattered rag- glared and spat. He cracked his whip. The ox, patient without hope, at once doomed and heroic, heaved. The wagon disappeared in the gloom.

A whisper of apprehension rose in her throat.

Wishing now she'd worn her wrap she gathered her collar around her. In the distance the bakery window beckoned; she crossed the cobblestones and went in. The warmth of the oven and the aroma of fresh bread surrounded her; behind the counter head lowered, stood the young woman, engrossed in a letter. Relieved, Gianna smiled and waved.

"*Ciao! Buongiorno!*"

The letter fluttered to the floor. The young woman turned, her cheeks streaked with tears, and Gianna saw her youth had vanished and her eyes were filled with loneliness and rage.

"May I help you?" said the woman, as if to a stranger. At the oven the old man scowled.

Unable to speak, Gianna shook her head and left.

Outside the fog had begun to lift. The sun emerged from the mist; in its sudden glare the buildings stood stark and naked, stripped of their subtle hues, ugly and crude. In the street a group of small boys huddled around a drain, dangling a piece of string. As Gianna hurried past, one of them – the wide-eyed boy from the bakery - looked up, his face a mask of worry and guilt. His fear struck like a serpent. She turned away, panic rising: in her path loomed a crooked figure, sweeping stones with his broom, flashing an idiotic grin. In the mirror of his lunatic gaze she glimpsed all at once the truth of what she had become: her compromises, her complicities. As if she herself had become the soothsayer, she felt the future flood into her; saw the inescapable fate of this small, fragile place held fast, all unknowing, in the cobra's gaze; heard the shouts of the Sturm Fuhrers, the rattle of tanks, the waves of violence to come. Her panic became rage: at the toothless fool; at the boy in the square; at the one-eyed gypsy; at her own life wasted, squandered in the company of spendthrifts, impostors and murderers.

The sun beat down. Her rage turned to regret. Her regret turned to shame.

The church bells rang. Heart pounding, she climbed the steps of San Bartolomeo Giusto and sought sanctuary in the shadows of the vestibule.

She found a pew and knelt but found herself unable to pray. From their niches along the nave the statues of martyrs hovered in silent reproach, proof of the vanity of life, the sorrows of mortal man, the lost promise of this unbearable Eden.

"Why so sad, my child?"

A figure stood over her, hands folded against his priestly robes. In his eyes she saw herself reflected as a child, an innocent girl in a communion dress.

The priest smiled. *"Perhaps I can be of help."*

His kindness was unbearable. She rose and with a cry pushed her way past him and fled, losing her heel as she rushed down the aisle, down the steps, out into the merciless glare.

BY EVENING the heat had abated. At Menucci's outdoor *caffè*, on a night lit with stars and the sparks from Menucci's smoke pots, a young woman sat by herself, her hair disheveled, shoes covered in dust, weeping into her napkin. For Gianna Massimi the day had brought only sorrow. Her spirit broken, she saw the world for what it was: a shattered promise, a paradise lost. With crystal clarity she understood that hope was an illusion, her life a meaningless charade. Realizing that, all of her feelings rose up and merged into one single feeling.

Grief.

At a table nearby sat a young man sipping a glass of fine chianti, compliments of a businessman who, somewhere across town, was just now realizing that his wallet, not to mention his tie clip, were missing. The young man watched the young woman dabbing at her eyes. Even from a distance her grief was palpable, almost as if it had heft and volume. As to the nature of the grief, there was no telling. Loss, betrayal, infidelity, disappointment, death: whatever the cause, it clung to her like an amulet of sorrow.

At least, so it seemed to Giuseppe Altamonte.

The napkin slipped from the girl's lap; in a flash he was on his feet, stooping to grab the napkin almost before it drifted onto the pavement.

"*Permette, Signora. Il vostro tovagliolo,*" he said, smiling.

She turned; he handed her the napkin and with a single, deft swipe of his hand, lifted from her the strands of her terrible grief.

And this was the remarkable thing: by the time Gianna had replaced the napkin on her lap, her tears had already begun to dry. Her sighs diminished; her absent smile returned. Reaching for her wine, as if suddenly reawakening to her surroundings, it occurred to her to thank the gentleman who had handed her the napkin; but by then, like all good thieves, he had left the scene.

She rose and paid her bill. In the moonlight she made her way across the piazza and back to her room where she washed away the dust of the day, then changed from her simple clothes into something more fashionable. She applied her makeup, put on her pearls, and became who'd she'd been. The following morning she called for her car and left, thinking, as she drove past the well, that with luck she could yet make her rendezvous in Capri.

She never again gave a thought to the place. Like a passing cold or a case of hay fever, it seemed hardly worth recalling.

EVENING

The moon, newly risen, peeks through the olive trees as the old man steps out his door. "*Benvenuta Luna, che mi porti fortuna!*" he calls. His voice, thin, reedy, like the creak of an oarlock, a rusty hinge.

The moon winks shyly and, salutations completed, begins her ascent.

Tip tip tap. Walking stick on paving stones, one shoe up, one down, the preposterous gait of a comical stork. Ludicrous to be old. Down the crooked path to the curb, the old man pauses, adjusts his cloak, sets his hat.

Which way?

"*Ciao, Senatore!*" Shouts from a trio of bicyclists passing close, heading uphill. More than three, in fact; in the failing light, hard to be sure. "*Where are you off to, old fossil?*"

"*None of your fucking business,*" he calls. Young people can be merciless in their bliss. Still, the girl looks familiar. And the boy. Emilio? No, Emilio died in the Great War. "*Don't forget to button your pants!*" Laughing, ringing their bells, the boys courageous as lions, the girls graceful as angels.

Renata, Aurora, Anna. Stefania

Which way? There. Down the hill toward the Piazza, the lights coming on in the square below. Too early for the *passeggiata*. *Bene*. So many people, pushing, the chatter, the noise; these days, the ruffians. Best to go straight to the bakery. One loaf, or two? Never mind, it's all on the list, which is in the hat.

The list is in your hat. Don't lose it, hear? Go straight to the bakery, then come right back. Carla, his granddaughter. Pain in the ass. Pretty, though. Smiles as she helps him on with his cloak. Little teeth, white as clouds.

Clouds. High in an endless summer sky. "*Gianni, sei il mio amore.*" *Gabriella.*

Sunlight pours through the hayloft door. Outside, the fields are alive. "Gianni, listen," she laughs, her voice husky with lust. "Hear how my heart is beating." Beneath their naked bodies the hay tickles their limbs. He licks the sweat from her belly, puts his ear to her chest, hears her heart, leaping, wild. "See what you do to me, Gianni?" She is his first. He knows he will marry her.

Gabriella, where are you now? Did you remember me? Did you grow old?

Her auburn curls spill like wine across the straw. Eyelashes flutter as he enters her again. Behind them, footsteps on the ladder. A face appears.

"Papà!" she cries, "Papà!"

Papà! Aspetta! Your hat! Papà! A man, waving, pointing. *Your hat! Eccolo!* The hat, a moment ago on top of his head, now dances on the sidewalk, tipped on one brim, spinning: an insolent acrobat. *Look at me!* The old man shuffles, stoops to pick it up; the hat scurries off, mocking, rolling, sailing upward on the breeze. *Catch me if you can!*

Piss on it.

Across the lane Baldelli the haberdasher plucks the hat from the air; in his hand it becomes once again just a hat. He crosses, sets it on the old man's head. "Careful, *Senatore*."

Fuck you, says the old man.

Baldelli laughs, pulls the hat down tighter. The moon, floating above a rooftop, crinkles her eyes in merriment. Six o'clock. Darkness falling. *Tip tip tap.* Around the corner into the Piazza. Nothing as it was. *Eccola.* The wheelwright's shop was there; here, the tavern. "*Gianni, fetch me a pint, before I beat you, subito, now!*" (Ten years later the bastard drools blood on his bed. "*Gianni, figliuolo, sweet boy, fetch me a pint.*" Gianni, now home from the sea, spits: drink this, old man.)

Now there are cars where once there were sheep. Everything else is gone: friends, enemies, heroes, shits, dogs, cats, lovers. Flown the coop. Last one out close the lights.

Tip tip tap. The list is in the hat. The bell on the bakery door tinkles; inside, a rush of noise, aroma, light. "*Buonasera.* What can I get you?" The young woman who runs the bakery. Such a face, lovely, soft. A child herself, she has a child. She smiles, asks questions, speaks too fast, too much noise, a small boy pushes past, almost knocks him over, out the door, "Niccolò!" she calls, but the boy is gone. "Did you bring a list?" she asks.

The list is in the hat. He looks. The list is not in the hat. The hat sailed up in the breeze.

"Don't worry, I know what to give you." She moves away, tightening her apron, a tiny waist. *Bella.*

Bella. Aurora, Anna. Stefania. Once there was a garden in which was a tulip in which was hidden a world. His head spins. He looks for a place to sit.

There. Next to the oven. The light is blinding. Leaping.

Fire!

Fire and heat. Below decks, the thrum of the engine room, the roar of the furnace, the throb of turbines, colossal. Stokers shoveling, arms aching, mountains of blackened coal. Next to him Pieter, grinning, dripping with sweat, a giant covered with soot, the shovel a toy in his hands. "*Gianni-boy, when we get to Trieste you will buy me a drink, many drinks, get drunk, many girls!*" Pieter, his friend from childhood. "*Fuck this place. We'll run away to Naples, work on the ships!*"

Pieter, whose skin turned to ash when the steam came in.

"*Ehi!*" A bird is singing. No, the woman in the bakery. She holds out the bread. "Does your daughter-in-law know you're out?" Once again he's an old man who means nothing. He takes the bag, tips his hat, goes through the door. Now there are people outside, *voicesvoicesvoices*, like the rumblings of trains through the Alps, like the screech of steel in the hold, like the screams of sailors, the sirens blaring –

"*Tenente! Wake up! Wake up, Lieutenant.*"

Stefania.

White blouse, collar starched, nurse's tray, changing the bandages, eyes like the soft edge of summer. "Does that hurt?" Stefania, nineteen, who gave him her heart, her soul. "*Sono tua, Gianni. You have all of me, since the day we met.*" Down from Trieste they escaped, together, through the olive groves, Chianti, Lambrusco, Trebbiano, aimless as gypsies, living like thieves,

Stefania, smiling in her sleep when he left, cowardly, sneaking down to the docks. *Good-bye Stefania. Do not think ill of me. Make up a story I died at sea.*

Now the tables are turned. *Now she will always be young, and I am old.*

Attento! Something is wrong. Someone has snatched his package, outside the bakery. *"S'matter, Geppetto, don't want to share your dinner?"* Four black-shirted *fascisti*, young men, passing the package around, over here over there. Thugs. He waves his stick, hits nothing, pathetic old fool. Once I would have smashed your skulls, danced on your eyes. They laugh, push, poke, grab his shoulders, spin him in circles. People walk by, look, say nothing: thugs, what can you do? *"C'mon, Gepetto, put up your dukes!"*

In Naples, he cut a man open with a shiv, blade grinding against the bone. *"Now you are a man, Gianni!" Pieter grinned.*

Now the world reels; down he goes, a broken puppet, strings sliced, hat flying, stick clattering. They fling the bread. Laughing, they leave. He lies there, in a stupid, undignified heap.

Doloroso ma non troppo. The big finish.

ENCORE!

Help him up! someone is saying. Hands reaching down, too many at once, pulling him up, brushing him off, replacing his hat, the stick, the bread, faces peering. *Okay, old man?*

Bene, bene. He has pissed himself, but no one sees. *Where are you headed?* they ask, hands pawing, groping.

The list is in the hat, he says.

The bakery woman from her door. *He lives on the hill! With his granddaughter!* She points; the jungle of hands turn him round like clay on a wheel. *That way old man.* Fuck you, he tells them. They laugh, and go away; why spend time on a thankless antique who smells like piss? "Who was he?" someone says. The others shrug, but one thinks he knows. *Fifty years. Important. Fought with Garibaldi. Lived over that way.*

Piss on them. Doesn't remember himself the place where he lived. Children all died in the Great War. Not the same after that. What does it matter? The bakery woman brings him more bread. Kind eyes. *Go home now* she tells him. *You live on the hill.* Which hill? The streets go every which way, ricky-ticky. He lives on the hill, but the hill is not home. Home was not on a hill, home was Renata, thirty-five years, flowered dress, flaxen hair, the cares of the world. *Gianni, look at us, wrinkles where we had dimples* she said, then died from the influenza. Children, how many? Six, seven, eight; one or two dead to start, the rest one by one dumped at sea, tossed in the ground, blown to bits in the war. No one left except for the granddaughter, Carla.

Come right back, she said.

He will not go back.

A group of small boys, squatting around a grate in the deepening dark, look up. "Why are you crying?" asks one.

Because I almost forgot, he says. "What are you looking for?"

"We're looking for something," says the boy. "*Stai zitto*," whispers another, who looks like the boy from the bakery. A string on his finger drops down through the grate. They are friends, complicit, intriguing; the elixir of immortality runs in their blood. Someday they too will forget. They will forget the beauty of the world.

The moon is over the Roman ruins. He will not go back. He will go to the ruins.

NIGHT. *Tip-tip-tap.* Across the square, past the shops, the *barbiere*, the *caffè*, the commerce of living, the stink of humanity, the warmth of argument, the pleasures of sex, the miracle of infancy, the sorrows of age. Past the hut of the stone-sweeper, what's his name? *Non importa;* one fool's the same as another, plenty of room on this earth for fools. Past the *cimitero* from whose wormy beds the remains of men he has admired, women he has kissed, beckon from beneath their pillows of stone. Gianni-boy!

Don't bother me. *I am on my way to the ruins.* Past the church, steeple spiking the sky. No, now not the church: the light has changed. A shadow, massive, ponderous, has heaved into view, blocking the moon. A ship! Lights agleam on the forecastle! An ironclad! The *thrump* of the pistons, the snarling of the screw. The warship "*Serpente*," wounded, listing, bow raised high, cut in half, the seas rushing in, at the end of her days.

Below decks, incendiary hell. Sirens wailing. *Fire!* The blast of the torpedo smashes his eardrums, rips the wrench from his hand. Shrapnel like a scythe. Arms, eyes, jaws, heads of men torn away. Water leaping through the breach like a hungry beast. A boiler bursts: a cyclone of scalding steam boils the bodies of those directly below. A cantata of screams; through the fog nothing, no one, can be seen.

Pieter! Pieter, where are you?

Above, the hatches slam and lock: now there will be no escape. Cries of despair, *Siamo perduti!* Another explosion rocks the ship. Water now swirling up to the waist.

Gianni! Over here! Hear, but cannot see. Struggling against the currents, breathing almost impossible. *Pieter! Over here!*

There is Pieter, the giant, his friend, looming up in the steam, waist deep, arms open wide, outstretched for a welcoming embrace. No, something else. The arms are crucified, pinioned, pierced, melted against a bulkhead. The chest is skewered by a falling pipe. The flesh, like suet, hangs loose from his face. *Gianni,* says the face, with something like a grin. *What's the worry? Life was for living, eh??*

The pipes explode. The face comes away. The soul goes up. Then a blast; the fire has reached the ammunition. The keel heaves and splits open; out through the gap tumbles seawater, flotsam, corpses – Gianni, alive! – into the brine, deep underneath.

(In the darkness, the old man huffs and scurries).

Above him the propeller spinning, barking, scraping, descends. The sound of giant footsteps, the hot breath of the past, chasing, seeking. His lungs on fire. He must come up. Endure.

Aspetta! Wait! Wait!!! In the shadows, out of breath, heart pounding, the old man stops. A tomcat screams; then, quiet. He leans against a stone.

He has reached the ruins.

Odysseus, home from the sea.

THE MOON, HAVING PASSED her zenith, curls onto her back and looks down patiently. The ground is frosted with light. The Roman ruins stand like iron blooms, a garden of stones, silent, unmoved since their fall a thousand years in the past. The rubble of history. *Barely rubble myself.*

Tip-tip-tap. Slowly now, each step a labor, he weaves among wrecked plinths and toppled archways toward the center of things: a pile of crumbling steps that rise, then stop, adjoining nothing. At their base, among weeds, flowers grow in riot: daisies, daffodils, tulips. *The world in a tulip.* The old man stops and looks. *I came here as a child. Now I am a child again.* He kneels into the flowers.

Gianni, where are you? Sunlight. Warmth. The buzzing of bees. Hidden among the blossoms, the perfume of lilacs, the rustle of breezes, Short pants. Stalks reaching up to his shoulders.

Gianni! Where are you hiding?

No one can see him. Not mother, not father, not God. Here is not here. Here is the earth before she received her name. He peers into the tulip, then falls, tumbling in, surrounded by petals. Ecstasy. Inside, a world of yellow, a world of light, infinite, untouched by evil, always happy, always safe, never hunger, never grief, never anger, never death, never sorrow, never regret.

Perdonami. Mother. Forgive me.

Aurora, Amalia, Stefania, forgive my arrogance, my cruelties, my selfishness, my callous wants, my blind assumptions. Forgive the sorrows of our youth, the scars of passion, the casual betrayals.

Perdonatemi.

My brothers and sisters, my friends; Pieter – especially you, Pieter; forgive my stubbornness. My selfish choice to survive when you did not, would not, could not.

Perdonatemi.

My children, whom I loved but could not protect, forgive my uncertain cruelties, my inattentions; forgive me your lives, your deaths, the murder of all your hopes.

Perdonatemi.

Renata, for whom there is nothing to be forgiven.

Perdonami.

God, I present you with my sins.

Addio.

Tip-tip-tap. The old man climbs the steps: one, two, three. Now he has become light as mist. His cloak slips from his shoulders; the cane clatters on the stones. The hat flies off. *Catch me if you can!*

At the top of the stairs, he is free.

The moon, her appointment kept, turns, languid, satisfied, and continues her slow descent.

The cloak, which held his sorrows, flutters to earth among the blooms.

The hat, ever antic, soars toward Andromeda.

HAT, CLOAK, and cane were discovered the following day, the hat dangling rakishly from Garibaldi's outstretched arm on Piazza Piccola. As to the old man, this was a mystery, as his body was never found. No one saw where he went.

Except, perhaps, Fausto.

Searching that night in the ruins for stones, Fausto watched as the old man climbed the crumbling stairs, and then climbed higher, up through the night, all the way to the moon. This he swore to Niccolò, on the condition that Niccolò never tell, lest people think Fausto a fool.

So, it remained a secret, to all but two.

And now you.

MORELLI'S HORSE

Another shadow, this time that of a cart.

The cart belonged to Octavio Morelli, seller of fruits and vegetables, a large man with a drooping mustache, the arms of a blacksmith, and a gentle soul. Each morning for seventeen years he and his horse bore the fruits of his garden to one particular spot in Piazza Piccola. There, spring, summer and fall, in sun and shade, wind and rain, Morelli sold his produce from the cart, while the horse stood patiently by. Everyone called Morelli Morelli. Everyone called the horse Morelli's Horse.

So, in a way, that was the horse's name.

Winters when there was less to grow and therefore less to sell, Morelli tended to his responsibilities at home, the labors of which had so far resulted in eleven children, all of them girls. And while it is not recorded how Signora Morelli felt about this remarkable feat, it was clear where Octavio stood: it was a great sadness of his life. Eleven girls in eleven tries! This for a man who was eighth of thirteen boys.

It wasn't that he didn't love his daughters, or work long hours to support them, or bring them gifts at Christmas, or sit beside them proudly at church on Sundays. The simple fact was that daughters were not sons, as Morelli's friends and neighbors were never loath to remind him.

"Still no rooster for the henhouse?"

"Forget to put the handle on the teacup, Octavio?"

"Looks to me like that pump needs a spigot."

Being the gentle soul he was, Morelli took these insults in good humor; at least, for the first few births. When, after four or five, no son had appeared, the barbs began to sting. After one or two more, the taunts became something else: advice.

"Eat meat," recommended Scarpacci the butcher.

"Face east at sunset," suggested Biggio the barber, who himself had several sons.

"A potion of garlic, codfish and toad," urged Allegretti the Socialist, who had it on authority.

"Prayer," intoned the priest Don Federico.

Accordingly, Morelli prayed, ate meat, faced east; drank garlic and codfish potions; even wore a rabbit's foot under his hat. Nothing worked. With each new arrival of ruby lips and flouncing curls, the fact grew more dismally profound: Morelli the vegetable seller had produced not one suitable gourd from his plantings. No one to farm with, to teach the ways of the garden, to bequeath the mysteries of manhood, to watch grow strong and straight, to lean on in his old age, to carry on his name.

Never once did Morelli complain. Still, over time, the benevolent smirks of his neighbors began to wear. Perhaps this is why Morelli turned for company to the one friend who could truly understand his plight: his horse.

Whose name, as we have established, was Morelli's Horse.

At dawn they could be seen silhouetted at garden's edge, Morelli traversing the rows, Morelli's horse waiting patiently in the traces as the cart filled with a cornucopia of ripening tomatoes, lettuce, carrots and celery. In the morning mist they walked to town past supple fields and rustic farmhouses, Morelli holding the lead even though Morelli's horse knew the way and had no need of it. Noontime they stood together in the rancorous bustle of the Piazza, exchanging goods for coins, nodding to neighbors and enjoying the occasional nap, one keeping watch while the other dozed in the hot sun. They stood together, ate together, endured the same flies together. Indeed, so much had people gotten used to seeing them standing head-to-head, it was often joked that Morelli and his horse were in the midst of conversation.

Which, often, they were.

"Rabbits," Morelli's horse would say, munching on an apple from his master's hand "are unruly, but determined. Give me any day the honesty of caterpillars, the insight of bumblebees."

To which Morelli, a man of few words, would nod, while counting out change for a customer. They discussed the firmness of the cucumbers, the state of the legumes, the vagaries of weather, the timing of cicadas, the latest rumors from the sheepcote. Occasionally, they debated human affairs.

"As to the politics of your *duce*, I remain unconvinced," said Morelli's horse. "Were I you, I would keep my eyes peeled for trouble. Blowhards like that have caused countless careless deaths."

"Young men by the millions," mused Morelli.

"In this case, I meant horses," yawned the horse, switching his tail at a horsefly.

Then there was the matter of Morelli's progeny. "He will need a name. A noble one," said the horse. This was at night, at home in the barn, while Morelli removed his harness. "A young man begins with his name."

"If he begins at all," replied Morelli, sipping from the flask he kept hidden in the straw.

"No one said it would be easy," said the horse. "Nothing comes from nothing, at least nothing worthwhile. This son of yours will need guidance, discipline; a strong hand, but gentle. Most of all, however, he will need a name."

"So you said," pointed out Morelli, sitting back in the straw and falling asleep.

"A noble one." repeated the horse, ignoring the fact Morelli was now snoring deeply. "He will see immense events. Encounter death by the thousands, both of your kind and mine. He will need a name to remember who he is, to avoid despair, to keep a fire within."

But Morelli heard none of this, lost as he was in a dream: of a thousand angry honeybees, in hot pursuit.

All of them girls.

IT HAPPENED THAT at that very same time in the very same town of Monte Castella, a young man, after a troubled and unpromising youth, had found his calling. Despite the fact he was neither big nor handsome nor gifted with grace, he had managed through cunning and betrayal to carve a place for himself in the politics of the moment, achieving a distinction for ruthlessness among the cadres of young men who had once spit upon him and whom he now meant to lead. He had developed swagger. Arrogance. He was given to unpredictable rage. He might have been seen as comical were the times not what they were.

As it was, people began to be wary of him. A little man. Pathetic. Dangerous. This man, whose name was Vincenzo Nutti, had taken to roaming Piazza Piccola in the company of three or four other young men, dressed in uniforms currently popular in Rome and Berlin. Projecting their youthful belligerence, they accosted passersby, occasionally flipping a cap or spilling a shopping basket, all the while shouting slogans, *"Me ne frego!"* *"Duce a noi! Credere, Obbedire, Combattere!"* Vincenzo, at their head, shouted loudest of all, his eyes alight with a thug's obscene power, excited by the lubricious thrill of seeing his own cowardice alive in others.

"Hooligans," growled Mamma.

Not everyone agreed. "So they're a little wild. *Ma che importa?*" said Bruno Fabbro to his wife, who was combing her hair and couldn't care less, "They represent our illustrious future."

"*Baggianate,*" spat Nonno. "It's a future like that that has sent my son to America."

Whatever the case it was only a matter of time before Vincenzo and his black-shirted *scagnozzi*, sniffing around for trouble, set their sights on Octavio Morelli and his cart, immobile in the center of the square. Braying their slogans, intent on drawing a crowd, the youths surrounded the cart,

212

plucking apples from the pile, while Morelli, always slow to anger, watched in silence, neither smiling nor frowning.

"*Cosa c'è*, vegetable man?" grinned Vincenzo, hoping to get a rise. "Don't you approve of *Duce*? Think you're better than everyone else?" He bit into an apple, spit it out. "*Spazzatura!* Garbage!"

"*Cinque centesimi,*" said Morelli.

Vincenzo turned to the small knot of people who had gathered. "Five cents!" he brayed. "For a piece of shit apple! What kinds of fools does he think we are? He wants us to pay for his turds?" He tossed a look to a comrade who reached for a melon and, with a sneer of contempt, dropped it on the pavement, where it splattered.

"*Quindici centesimi,*" said Morelli.

The color rose in Vincenzo's pitted cheeks. "You hear that?" he called. "The more he screws us, the more the price goes up! Just like the enemies of the *Patria!* Bastards! Cheats! Traitors! Yids! "

Another melon hit the pavement. "*Trenta centesimi,*" said Morelli.

The knot of observers had become a small crowd. Now Vincenzo, his rage becoming exquisite, stepped up to Morelli, who towered over him.

"Seems to me you're a cheat yourself. A bastard and a cheat. Is that right?"

Morelli stood, unmoving, his eyes locked with Vincenzo's. He said nothing.

"*Viva il Duce!*" shouted Vincenzo, sending spittle onto Morelli's coat. "Say it!"

Morelli said nothing.

The young man's fury had reached the boiling point; perhaps because of this, he had failed to notice a movement directly behind him, a shift in position by Morelli's horse. Instead of facing the cart, the horse's rump was now pointed directly at Vincenzo Nutti.

"Say it," he hissed to Morelli. "*Viva Il Duce!* Say it. Loud!"

With that, the horse let loose: a long, loud, rolling, thundering fart, rich in the aroma of oats, resonant with the scent of sarcasm, exploding within inches of Vincenzo's head.

The crowd erupted in laughter. The horse switched his tail. The laughter grew. Helpless, undone by a horse, Vincenzo looked around for some way to salvage his pride. His eye lit on the cart.

"Tip it," he ordered. When the blackshirts hesitated, he grabbed the traces himself. "Tip it!" he howled. In a matter of seconds the cart sat overturned, contents spilling helter-skelter across the cobblestones. Still, the crowd kept laughing. Vincenzo trembled with fury.

"We'll see what's funny, when the time comes," he announced, and stalked away, laughter ringing in his ears, his entourage scrambling to keep up.

By that evening the tale of the fart that saluted the *Duce* had spread across the Piazza, causing a good deal of quiet merriment. There was, however, reason for caution.

"You'll want to be careful," said the horse as they made their way home among the soft songs of birds and the lullaby of the crickets. "We've made an enemy of that kid."

"He'll get over it," shrugged Morelli.

"Don't count on it," snorted Morelli's horse.

But Morelli couldn't worry: he had more pressing issues at hand. A child was expected, any day.

THE CHILD WAS BORN a girl, and took her place alongside the eleven others on Morelli's knee. Admittedly, a setback. Still the next night, Morelli's horse was optimistic. "Life has its trials. This is yours."

"Apparently," mumbled Morelli, flask in hand. "Talk to me about something else."

"The barn mice predict further trouble from Rome. There are rumors of impending disaster, though that might be local," mused the horse.

"The barn mice are their own worst enemy," noted Morelli, and fell asleep in the hay, flask in hand.

Had the vegetable seller been less drunk, therefore more careful about where he set down his lantern, there might be nothing further to report from that evening; as it was, the fire that devoured the barn very nearly turned Morelli's twelve ruby-lipped daughters into orphans overnight. Indeed, his survival hinged on the actions of his horse, who braved the inferno twice: once to save himself, then going back to retrieve his owner.

"You saved my life." Morelli said the next day.

"You're welcome," rasped Morelli's horse. But while the vegetable seller's injuries were nothing more than scalds and burns, the horse suffered worse. The smoke he'd inhaled was gone, but the fire still burned in his lungs.

"I'll put you to pasture," offered Morelli.

"Nonsense. There is work to do."

"The work can wait."

"Time is running out," said the horse, rising wearily from the straw "And we have yet to choose a name."

And well enough was Morelli's horse to rise again each morning and stand at the garden's edge giving thanks to the dawn while the cart slowly filled; to journey to town past fields and farms he had known since he was a colt; to savor the smell of the turnips, the creak of the cart, the sacred rustle of the leaves, to know as only creatures of the earth can that his burden had been beloved, his labors fulfilled. To stand, stertorous, rasping, amid the bustle of the square, always turning in his mind the issue at hand.

This went on for many weeks until a day in early summer when, at the entrance to the piazza, suddenly and to his own surprise, the horse went down on his knees and sighed.

"I'm near the end," said Morelli's horse, as Morelli cut loose the traces.

A crowd gathered, curiosity mixed with impatience: a fallen horse was both a pity and a nuisance. A line of wagons and carts began to form at the entrance, unable to pass. Attempts to persuade the horse to move proved unsuccessful. Someone suggested a whip, but Morelli declined. The crowd grew larger; the line grew longer. An argument broke out between Renzo the coalman and Nucci the ironmonger as to whose cargo commanded right of way.

At the door of the bakery Niccolò, sweeping the floor, watched as from the rear of the line, a large black automobile barged forward, horn sounding, and stopped just short of the horse and cart. A young man, black shirted, booted and holstered, stepped from the car

"What's the holdup?" barked Vincenzo Nutti. "Who is responsible for this?"

"It's the horse, Section Leader Nutti," shouted Fabbro the stablemaster, who had been watching from a distance. "He's blocking traffic. Someone should do something."

Vincenzo, aware all eyes were on him, spun on his heel to take in the problem. His eyes lit on Morelli. A smile appeared, reptilian. "Your horse?" he inquired pleasantly, though of course he knew.

"My horse," said Morelli.

"Move him."

Morelli glanced at the horse. "Perhaps in a moment," he said.

"I have an appointment," said Vincenzo. "Get him out of the way, before I lose patience."

Morelli considered this. Considered the warnings of the mice.

"*Viva Il Duce,*" he said.

From the horse came a sound; a whinny; a bray. To some, it sounded like laughter. Vincenzo reached for his pistol.

"You mock," he said, and put the gun to the head of Morelli's horse, who looked toward Morelli.

"Primo," said Morelli's horse. "The boy's name will be Primo."

Vincenzo pulled the trigger. The shot was loud. The horse keeled over, dead. Vincenzo stepped back.

"Let that be a lesson," he smiled. He strutted back to his car.

"FINITA LA MUSICA." A garden has no time for sorrow. By spring Morelli's cart again travelled the road to Piazza Santa Caterina Piccola, pulled by a strong young bay who had a name but little interest in the gossip of birds, earthworms and mice. This horse and Morelli never spoke. There was no need; deep in the winter before, while rain pelted the fields and the turnips all slept, there arrived to Morelli, thanks in part to his wife, a child; the thirteenth. A boy. A son.

There was no question as to a name.

Primo Morelli would live to see immense events; to encounter death by the thousands, of both horses and men. Through it all he would remember who he was, avoid despair and, true to his father's instructions, keep a fire within. For reasons not fully understood, he loved the rustle of the leaves.

And, he would travel.

As would Niccolò.

THE SECRET

Once again that winter the cold rains arrived in Monte Castella, but Niccolò no longer woke to the comforting heat of the oven below. He slept in his own room now, above the storeroom, and rose to his chores in the morning chill. Nevertheless he was still a little boy, and once a week, when the letter from America arrived, he nestled in Mamma's arms to hear her read.

Papà was working now at a shipyard; the bakery job he'd been promised months ago had not yet come through. But those ships! The mighty steamers, funnels belching as they passed the Statue of Liberty. A magnificent sight! Papà loved the Statue of Liberty. To him, it meant freedom.

But to Niccolò, it meant something else.

Skip that part, Mamma, he would say, go on to the next. And she would, thinking the boy was merely bored. But his mind would not go on: it stayed behind, restless, fretting, until it could not be contained. Against all his wishes, it would fly from his head, out into the darkness, to the spot across the Piazza where the terrible secret lay; in a hole in the street, beneath the grate, wedged in a fissure, out of reach. The severed head, torn from her body, eyes staring upward in silent accusation.

The statue. Broken.

The gift from Papà. Lost.

Guilty.

—◦—

"YOU COULD GET IT," Rinaldo said as they squatted above the iron grate where Niccolò had gone nearly every day since the statue had fallen from his pocket. Niccolò had tried everything to retrieve it, but at summer's end, nothing had worked – the head was firmly wedged, immoveable.

"This drain empties down at the river. Sooner or later it'll end up there. When things dry up you could go find it."

"You think so?" said Niccolò, doubtful.

"*Assolutamente*," said Rinaldo. But no one trusted Rinaldo any more.

The head stayed put, while the rest of the corpse lay hidden behind sacks of flour in the storehouse. When Mamma asked where the statue had gone, Niccolò said he had it hidden away for safekeeping, then quickly changed the subject. She just nodded. It was the first lie he had ever told her.

And to make things worse, Mamma had stopped singing.

"First six months, then another year. Still he's not ready. When will he send for us? Does he understand what's happening here? Does he want us at all?" Mamma sat with Nonno going over the bills. Niccolò eavesdropped from the doorway. It was true that things were happening on the piazza. Walls once bathed in smoky afternoon light now stood covered by angry images: posters, slogans, clenched fists and the bellicose leer of *Il Duce*. As for Papà, the unsettling truth was that sometimes Niccolò could hardly remember him at all: how he looked, how he was. Not like Quindici's father, who beat Quindici with his belt, or Rinaldo's, a stonemason, big men with hands like cudgels and voices like falling rocks who wiped their mouths with their sleeves and smelled of beer and manure. Not even like Nonno, who was lean and tough, like leather stretched over wire. Papà, he thought, stood straight and tall. A moustache that tickled. But of his voice, Niccolò had almost no recollection; it was Mamma who spoke his words for him. And now Mamma was worried.

When would he send for them? Niccolò thought of the ships in the harbor, the magnificent steamers. Perhaps, surrounded by such wonders, Papà had simply forgotten them – Mamma, Niccolò, the bakery, the little piazza.

Or perhaps it was something else.

Niccolò thought of another night, at the end of the summer; the sudden rain in the square. How, shrouded in mist, she had appeared, neither with torch nor robes, but startling in her nakedness. Then she was gone. Now Mamma cried at night in her room and Papà worked on ships, far away.

He had to do something. But now it was winter. Niccolò would have to wait.

Maybe something would happen.

THEN THEY WERE ON A TRAIN.

Niccolò stood between seats, nose pressed to the window, the winter landscape flashing by, whole towns revealed and discarded in the blink of an eye, further by far than he'd ever been from home. Next to him sat Mamma, dressed in Sunday clothes, their bag on the rack above them. Across from her, facing her, was the man. Dark, mustached, erect, wearing a uniform. He was smiling.

A Roma? Bene!

Just overnight, said Mamma. To get a *passaporto*.

The man frowned. *Leaving Italy?*

Maybe, she said.

Why? So beautiful here. Like yourself.

Mamma looked away. The train sped on.

Outside the sky darkened. The window, now opaque, turned its face and looked inward. Niccolò saw his own face reflected; then Mamma's, smiling secretly. Then the man, watching Mamma. The man didn't know Niccolò could see.

When they returned home Niccolò stood up in school and told of his trip: the train, the Roma Termini, the trolley to the passport office, the blackshirts and soldiers all around; how he slept, hurtling through the night, all the way home.

"Now you are a world traveler," laughed la maestra Leonora. "Ready for your trip to New York. When will you go?"

"I don't know," Niccolò said. "Papà won't say."

He never mentioned the man in uniform who had stayed on the train and gone with them and helped with the *passaporti*, then patted Niccolò on the head, bowed to Mamma and clicked his heels.

But when they got home, he heard Mamma singing again.

THE NATURAL STATE of a young boy isn't worry, but hope. With the coming of spring the doors of Niccolò's life flew open again, the dark dreams of winter pushed aside by the promise of new adventures. In New York the job Papà had been promised had at last come through; now he was working in a place he admired, putting money aside. Soon, he promised, he would send for Niccolò and Mamma. Still, Mamma shook her head.

"Soon?" she said. "When is 'soon'?"

"*Presto è presto,*" Nonno shrugged. "Be patient."

Mamma rolled her eyes, and wiped her hands on her apron.

On Piazza Piccola the winter rains washed the stones clean, making way for the dust and dung of summer. Fausto emerged from his winter hibernation to repair the fallen stones of his hut. In the evenings the *passeggiata* resumed, made delightful by the perfume of April blossoms. Around the statue of Garibaldi debris from the winter runoff had filled the grate with sticks and mud. Peering down, Niccolò saw no sign of Liberty's head. The crime, it now seemed, had been washed away to the river.

Now there were chores in the afternoons. After school Niccolò worked in the bakery sweeping the floors and helping Nonno fetch supplies from the storeroom. For this Niccolò received his own apron, of which he felt proud. Someday, Nonno said, the boy would join his father, working the oven in their new bakery across the sea. Things, it seemed might be all right.

223

Still there was a loose end that remained, one place in the storeroom that Niccolò had avoided: in the very back, where the ceiling drooped low and the air never moved and the light hardly penetrated; the place where long ago last fall he had hidden the broken torso of the statue in a niche behind the tins of cooking oil and preserves. Every day as he fetched sacks of flour, Niccolò could sense it, a helpless wrack, its arm still raised in a pathetic, now meaningless salute, pointing toward the boy who had been entrusted with its care. Sooner or later, Niccolò would have to dispose of it; then it could be forgotten. After all, things were different now. It had been months since Mamma had even asked.

Now was the time.

He chose a day when Nonno was busy at the oven and Mamma was serving customers at the counter. Niccolò entered the empty storeroom. Ducking low, watching for mice, he moved to the back, feeling his way to the tins and jars. Bending forward, he reached into the niche.

The niche was empty.

In an instant he knew. His secret had been discovered. In an instant, the world crashed around him. He understood.

Mamma knew. Nonno, Papà as well. All winter they'd watched him, knowing he'd lied, their disappointment growing by day. If they knew this, what else had they found about his secret store of shame? Scarpacci's wife; Maestra Leonora's bottom; the Virgin Mary; Liberty's head, trapped in the grate beneath Garibaldi; the dizzying spiral of guilt and shame and confusion that had swallowed him up and now stripped away forever their pride in him.

No wonder Mamma had stopped singing.

His only wish at that moment was to stay forever there in the dark, out of sight of the world, entombed behind sacks of flour; to climb into the niche

224

and hide until world's end. But Niccolò was a boy, and the world was very old; it might last for a long time. Then he would miss his bed, and the bakery, and Mamma's embrace, and Nonno, and the trees, and the endless blue sky. Were all those things already lost to him? Even now was he falling to Hell?

From the front of the store he heard Mamma's laughter. A desperate hope rose up. Perhaps even now there was a chance for salvation. If he was brave, if he confessed, perhaps it could be all right. When he had gathered his courage, he inched toward the storeroom door, then climbed the two steps into the bakery.

After the dark of the storeroom, the light pouring through the front windows made him squint. Silhouetted at the counter stood Mamma, wiping her hands on her apron, her laugh cascading like a waterfall. Across from her, in a dark coat, hands in his pockets, stood Papà. Tall, handsome, smiling.

Only, not Papà.

The man from the train.

And Mamma was laughing. No one else was in the bakery. She hadn't seen him come in.

He ran.

"Niccolò!" called Mamma.

But Niccolò was already out the door.

THE STREAM, one of several that flowed from the hills, cut through a wooded ravine that skirted the edge of Monte Castella. In early spring the water, clear and cold, tumbled against the rocks, filling the air with a chorus of murmurs and shouts. A series of crumbling steps led down to a pebbled beach along the stream, littered with sticks and branches, papers, the bones of small birds, sometimes more, including the runoff from the storm drains in the town up above.

Niccolò, capless, coatless, descended. He had never been here at this time of year, and never by himself. Mamma forbade it; many were the stories of children carried off by rogue currents, only to appear as bloated corpses in the nets of fisherman far below at entrances to the sea. But that was before; now things were different. He had heard Mamma's calls from the doorway as he raced from the bakery; the shouts from Quindici and the others as he ran past them without stopping, gasping for air, choking back his tears. Now, as he reached the darkness at the bottom of the ravine, all that seemed long ago. Now he was one thing, alone, condemned, the poison of his father's loins and the womb of his mother, who was not a virgin, but who smiled at the man on the train, who was not his father.

He needed to find the statue's head and make things right.

Along the bank the fallen branches bent beneath his feet. In the rushes the remains of tin cans clung like nestlings. A mitten, decayed; a serving spoon; the rusted bell of a gramophone. Everywhere Niccolò looked lay artifacts of despair. He was sure he would never find her.

And then, in the stream, a light flashing beneath the surface, caught in an eddy, spinning. Another flash! Too far out in the current to be sure; still, only a few steps, the water not so deep there, if the footing could hold.

She had come to him in the rain, now she was calling again. One step, the water across his shoes, achingly cold. The stones more slippery than they looked. Six more steps, perhaps he could reach. The water, yelling, snarling, determined not to give up its prize, nipping at his legs; the cold now stiffening, the light still flashing in the eddy. Papà would be proud.

Another step. Then, the stones dropped away. From beneath, the river reached up, seized him, spun him down. He reached for the flash; grasped at nothing.

That was the last he saw of the light.

———

NEWS OF THE BOY'S accident spread like lightning across the Piazza; by evening a crowd had gathered at the bakery. Already an authoritative account of what had happened – based on rumor, surmise and wishful thinking – had circulated among the populace. Niccolò's life had been spared, depending on who was asked, by an angel, an otter, a fisherman with a halo. A less spectacular version credited the rescue to the boy's grandfather, who had followed Niccolò to the stream and seen the boy tumble in. This version was largely ignored.

The critical fact was that the boy was alive though he'd very nearly drowned. He was suffering but was sure to make a full recovery. This was announced to the crowd by Signor Alberto Morosco, an old army friend of Niccolò's father who, as it happened, had been in town to deliver passports to the baker's wife and child, and who had assisted in pulling Niccolò from the torrent. The mother, meanwhile, as mothers do, blamed herself, though everyone who knew her knew of course that was nonsense: a woman so caring, and cheerful, and pretty, could hardly be blamed.

As to the object clutched in the boy's hand there continued to be confusion. Some said it was the head of a bronze figurine: others, simply a shiny stone. Whatever the case, it no longer mattered; at least, not to Niccolò.

For here was the odd truth: the boy who went into the torrent that afternoon, confused and frightened, was not the same as the boy who came

227

out. In the roll and tumble, the grip of the icy blackness, something had spoken; the mysteries became clear, the pieces knitted together. The world – incomprehensible, coincident, bright with magic – showed itself to him, and made sense. Now, alone in his bed beneath blankets, surrounded by sounds and objects he loved – the tick of the oven, the smell of the bread, the rasp of Nonno's grumbling and Mamma's lilt, the particular slant of light through the window of the place which had nurtured him since birth – Niccolò knew something had changed forever. In the stream he had been places he never knew existed; now he could never come back. Despite Mamma's arms, home meant something else.

In his mind, he saw tall spires, the rush of autos, the push of big trains.

A new world.

Papà.

The gleam of Liberty.

America!

1 9 4 5

Now let the shadow be that of a young soldier.

The soldier stands in the center of a once-busy square beneath another hot summer sun, gazing up at a cloudless sky. He is twenty years of age. He wears a uniform and carries a rifle. All around him there is dust and rubble and the tracks of tanks and the bones of horses, although not just horses. In the distance can be heard the sound of big guns, but here is silence. What happened in this place is done.

He has come up a road from the valley below; before that on a troopship across an ocean; before that from the city where he went with his mother to join his father a lifetime – twelve years – ago. Before that time, from the moment of his birth, everything and everyone he knew and ever loved came from this place.

Now this place is gone.

The Grand Hotel Imperiale. The movie theater, the vegetable cart. The bakery where his grandfather baked bread. His grandfather as well. Only the church remains, pitted and smashed, and the Roman ruins beyond, which were ruins before. Otherwise, the past is unrecognizable. All that occurred, or might have occurred, or didn't; all that was possible then.

Piazza Santa Catarina Piccola. All of that noise.

Great sorrows are mute.

A stirring in the rubble; the soldier whirls and raises his weapon. From the stones appears a face. An aviator's cap. A flag, tied to a broomstick.

"*Americano?*"

"Fausto?"

Snaggle-toothed, covered in dust, Fausto rises and salutes. Sweeper of stones, commander of rubble.

"Where are the others?" calls Niccolò.

Fausto looks around as if he's just noticed, shrugs. "*Andati. Tutti andati.*"

Gone where? Fausto, do you remember? The voice in the well? The *caffè*? The scent of argument and manure, rising up to heaven from this most and least heavenly place?

Fausto shrugs. "*Non mi ricordo.*" Not even the fool recalls.

The soldier turns to go. Then, a light in the other man's eyes.

"*Aspetta! Wait!*" he calls.

Niccolò turns back. Fausto raises his arm and points across the devastation, to the spot where, above a storm drain, the statue of Garibaldi stood. Only scattered shards remain. Fausto's face is alive with joy.

"Qui si fa l'Italia o si muore," he calls, laughing.

Here we make Italy, or die.

From up the hill, on a breeze, comes the tinkling of a piano.

THE END

CPSIA information can be obtained
at www.ICGtesting.com
Printed in the USA
LVHW072001180722
723787LV00015B/205/J

9798986306902